ORIGINS

CURVE
OF
HUMANITY

BOOK ONE

MAQUEL A. JACOB

Cover art by:

Keith Johnston

https://keithdraws.wordpress.com

Edited by:

Rhiannon Rhys-Jones

Published by MAJart Works

www.majartworks.com

Hillsboro, Oregon

BOOKS BY MAQUEL A. JACOB

THE CORE TRILOGY

CORE OF CONFLICTION: BOOK 1

SEEDS OF CONVICTION: BOOK 2

BONDS OF CONTRITION: BOOK 3

WELCOME DESPAIR

A COLLECTION OF SHORTS

BLOOD DOCTRINE

COMING SOON

CURVE OF HUMANITY

BOOK TWO: SHADOWMEN OBJECTIVE

BOOK THREE: PURGE SEQUENCE

BOOK FOUR: CRIPPLED EARTH

BLOOD DOMINION

(BOOK TWO OF BLOOD DOCTRINE)

ACKNOWLEDGEMENTS

Thank you for taking a chance on my new six book series Curve of Humanity. My great passion is to find the good in humanity and show we can combat corruption within our societies. This book series is a lesson of hope in the face of futility.

Or so I would like to think.

For those who encouraged me to keep going when it all seemed too daunting, I appreciate you all. To the early stage beta readers: Theresa Walton, Monica Callahan, and Mom, my sincere condolences and immense gratitude. Your enthusiasm and no holds barred feedback is priceless.

A huge thanks to NaNoWriMo (National Novel Writing Month) for supporting writers' creative juices. My peeps at NIWA, you all keep my humble and showed me to put myself out there with no fear.

Sarah Walker and John Howard, two awesome writing buddies who helped hone my craft along with Sean Hoade (you're a hot mess and I love you dearly). Voss Foster, you rock for helping me out in a pinch.

To Jason V. Brock for making me turn the dial in my brain and retrain it. Sunni Brock, you are a ray of sunshine. Thank you, William F. Nolan for constantly telling me not to quit; to keep writing and keep learning.

Keith Johnston: Your talent is mind blowing. I never thought the covers would turn out so awesome. Look forward to working with you again on future projects.

CHAPTER ONE

A Sonnet for Humanity

-Blind Sheep-

I had hope for some sense of sanity
It being the 21st century of man
But, it seems we are losing our humanity
With no way of fixing it- If we can.
The end is near, or so they say
They, being the prophets and pessimists
Salivating at the promise of doomsday
Even as society and everyday life persists.
Let us not fall in line
Marching towards our own annihilation
And read into the inevitable sign
Of our final destination
Lest we forget an important note
We all wear the same human coat.

- Rachel E. Robinson 2012

FORCED ENTRY

Beams of red and yellow streaked across the vast darkness of space engulfing their targets in fireball explosions. The void bore silent witness to two alien armadas exchanging violence for the sole purpose of annihilation, with both sides suffering massive losses as the battle raged on. Eighty League ships pitted themselves against one hundred of the Relliant Command fleet.

Captain Darnizva stood rooted at the center of his League ship's command deck watching the vid screens above the observation panel. His crew remained calm, switching to emergency engines, and deploying more squadrons while weathering the tremors from the bombardment of Relliant fire due to its position on the front lines. He frowned at the data flooding across the holoscreen floating in front of him. Klaxons rang throughout the corridors pinpointing the damage. The overhead auxiliary lights flickered, signaling an inevitable loss of power. Warriors pulled double duty defending the ship and assisting the medical teams with extractions. This battle would not be won today by either race.

We have to jump.

There was no question of that, just a matter of when. Timing was key. A bad jump would mean losing all. His ship could haul seven command ships from the front lines along and with those four others. The main fleet would undoubtedly jump back to their home world, Karysilan.

"Prepare to lock on the guidance systems for the ships in our perimeter and align a route on the galactic pathways."

"Sir?"

The navigator's head snapped up from studying his workstation's screen.

"Did I not make my instructions clear?"

"Yes, Sir!" His fingers maneuvered across the console at high speed.

This is the only way to survive right now.

Captain Darnizva stepped back and leaned against the command post. Because he was in front, instead of behind it, the curved metal pressed against his spine. Hooking both arms around under the bars to use as an anchor, he braced for what would be nothing short of a crash landing. For even as the ship entered the opened pathway, enemy fire made contact; violently knocking the ship into an angled position.

A vortex opened wide as the front hull of the first ship emerged into the unknown solar system. As it slowed down, two heavily crippled ships sped past from both sides. More came through in various arrays of damage, the ones unscathed maneuvering out of the way towards the dark side of a nearby planet. There was no way for the damaged ships to decelerate, leaving the Commanders of seven ships to watch in horror as the other five, engulfed in flames, plummeted towards the blue and white planet ahead.

On the surface of planet Earth, its inhabitants went about their daily lives, none the wiser to the calamity about to come knocking. The exceptions were eight scientists from different countries who collaborated on a joint extraterrestrial investigation stemming from the Roswell incident twenty-three years prior. Although the claims were debunked, they decided to keep looking and go deeper. They had become their own power over the decades and even governments feared them.

A constant vigil was set up to watch the skies 24/7 and on this day, only a week after Thanksgiving, they were getting an early Christmas present.

1974

Professor Pretchov sucked in air at a rapid pace, trying not to hyperventilate, as he ran down the corridor to the viewing room. He was tall, slender, over forty and out of shape. Sweat had already drenched the front of his shirt and his face in the two minutes he had traveled. His white lab coat floated back flipping side to side. One of the observers had called not fifteen minutes ago to inform him of large images spotted just outside Earth space. Almost instantly, he and his organization began confirmation with their own facility's sightings. The broadcast equipment was already being set up so they could communicate with each other in real time.

He burst through the double doors and was greeted with chaos. A cacophony of noise filled the room with the decibel level getting higher. The computers clacked and clicked, alarms sounded, hard copy data feeds were being spewed out of the printers. Yelling. Lots of excitement mixed with terror. On the large monitor, he saw the blown-up image of the objects coming towards them at high speed. There was no doubt about what they were. Those ships were not from Earth. Watching the feed, they all saw smaller vessels emerge from the larger ships, some exploding before disintegrating as they attempted what appeared to be evacuation. Professor Pretchov winced and a gasp of sadness resounded in the room.

"Professor." One of his lab technicians tapped him. "Professor."

"Hmm?"

He turned to the tech and looked behind him.

"We're ready to broadcast."

Turning to the screens set up in a semicircle against the back wall, he saw each one flicker to life, revealing his comrades. In the background of each scene, he noticed similar forms of chaos, excitement and awe. The eight scientists acknowledged one another with a nod and waited for more information from their technicians. Professor Lancaster from the United States was the first to state the obvious.

"If you notice, gentlemen and ladies, some of those ships coming towards us are severely damaged. Our planet will not come out of this unscathed. The impact will devastate whatever territory they crash in. It is too late for evacuation procedures. Our government has decided to shut down all media to prevent mass panic and afterwards will state it was an unprecedented meteor storm. Per my suggestion, of course."

Professor Makoto of Japan chimed in.

"The same has occurred in my country as well. It seems no one wants to believe we are about to come in direct contact with other beings."

"From the trajectory of the ships, I believe they will hit five different continents. One will definitely hit the ocean and cause a tsunami like nothing we have ever seen," the female professor of Italy, Dr. Morandi, concluded.

"We must contain the crash sites immediately. There can be no access for anyone except who we choose."

Professor Pretchov paced the floor as he talked. "The fact that our governments laughed at us all those years ago. Giving us full authority on this kind of situation without thinking it a possibility is to our advantage."

"Since we now have the full control and backing of our governments, we need to get accurate coordinates for the crash sites and get our people on the ground within hours, if not minutes," Professor Headland of Australia suggested.

"Not so fast, gentlemen." Professor Muller of Russia interrupted. She wagged her finger at the screen. "We must first know if there is radioactive backlash. Our hazmat protocols may not be enough. We are talking about an Alien injection into our ecosystem."

The others nodded in agreement. They had to ensure it was safe to enter the zone before anything. For all they knew, the ships' material could be toxic and capable of wiping out the entire human race. Loud gasps erupting in unison from the technicians behind the monitors made the scientists turn to their own viewing screens. It had begun. There was no room for error or panic. Each viewing lab was built underground and even though the facilities would hold, they were going to get severely shook.

"Whoever gets their hands on any of the surviving smaller ships needs to establish containment procedures. They may be hostile, but I doubt that. I have a feeling our planet was not their destination." Professor Pretchov turned back to his colleagues' distressed faces. "Every living soul on the planet will see them coming within the next twelve hours."

"May God have mercy on our government leaders' souls for not alerting the public," Professor Lancaster said while making the sign of the cross on his chest.

With the broadcast meeting ended, equipment was packed up in preparation for the move to the lower levels. There was a horrid feeling permeating the lab stemming from not being able to notify family or friends. There would be nothing they could do even if they did. What was about to occur seemed to be taken right out of a movie. He was sure many of his techs wished it were. Hell, so did he. Taking one last glance at the viewing room, Professor Pretchov wiped his face in a downward motion with one hand then followed the rest of his crew.

⌢

Giant balls of fire lit up the sky as they descended, forcing people to look up in awe, then terror. Cars stopped mid traffic, market squares halted transactions, and air traffic control around the world declared an emergency requesting aircrafts not to land for as long as possible. Places of worship became overcrowded with people on their knees praying to their gods for redemption and safety. Not even martial law could combat the mass hysteria that swelled as imminent impact closed in. There would be no mercy.

In Italy, one of the large ships tore through an entire city, stopping only when it was embedded so deep into the ground, the debris caved in to cover it. Another ship made impact in the Arabian Desert, burrowing deep into the sand. An entire forest in the United States was wiped out and a new canyon formed around the damaged ship before collapsing on top of it. Massive earthquakes destroyed fault lines, creating new bodies of land.

As one ship hit the Pacific Ocean, the ripple effect spread along the shorelines of surrounding continents.

Steam hotter than an inferno and thick as smoke filled the air from the fiery mass contacting water. Beaches disappeared along with any structure within eighty miles of the giant waves. Aquatic life was either disintegrated or boiled to death. All this before the water began to recede back.

The fifth ship crashed into Russia far inland off the Kara Sea, its speed and weight carrying it down into the ground along with a third of Noril'sk and its people. Professor Pretchov, sitting in a bunker on the outskirts of Moscow with his technicians, felt the crash and realized they were not prepared for the aftershock as they had originally thought. But one thing kept him elated despite equipment being tossed and crew members screaming in agony from being impaled or crushed; one of the ships had landed in his backyard. A smile crossed his face as the main power grid failed.

⤺

From above, the scene looked gruesome. Professor Morandi peered down at what was once a great city and pursed her lips in regret. The military helicopter had to fly low enough for her crew to witness the site but high enough not to get caught in the debris filled air. A recovery team was already at work searching for bodies and a salvage unit was combing through the wreckage for anything useful. The European Center for Disease Prevention and Control, had cleared the crash site only a few hours ago but the Professor wanted to get the ball rolling quickly. If excavation was not possible, they could at least try to analyze the ship's structure material.

"Why are they searching for bodies? Nothing could have survived that intact," one of her lab technicians spoke, breaking the heavy silence.

"Don't you have any hope?" A female tech snapped. "Why are you being so pessimistic?"

He nodded towards the window, gesturing her to see for herself.

"You tell me."

Tears filled her eyes but she didn't look out. Instead she turned away from the horrific scene and wrapped her arms around herself. Professor Morandi almost pitied the girl. She was one of the younger scientists and still a little green.

"Where would you like to land, Professor?"

The pilot's voice crackled in her ears.

"There."

Professor Morandi pointed to a clearing a little over a mile from the crater. They could use the exercise and time to think while they trekked to the edge. This was an experience of a lifetime and she was not going to let her conscience or morality get in the way. She could deal with that later.

"Roger that," the pilot confirmed.

The helicopter tilted sideways and maneuvered towards the clearing. It leveled off to hover above the scorched ground before landing. Professor Morandi barely waited for the blades to stop spinning as she hurried out. The ground beneath her feet crumbled to ash, sending up tiny puff clouds. A strange odor filled the air and just as she was about to identify it, one of her techs announced it.

"Oddio! It smells like death to the highest power!"

A few of the crewmembers covered their mouths while two techs coughed and vomited. Getting used to the smell wouldn't be easy. They all looked over at the mass crater and stood mesmerized by its size. There was a reason it took out an entire city; its size appeared equal.

"This could take years!" One of the male techs

exclaimed. "Decades!"

"Yeah," an older male scientist next to him replied. "Isn't it spectacular?"

Professor Morandi let the smile on her face widen. *Spectacular indeed.*

❧

Professor Lancaster stared wide eyed at the motionless figure being gently laid on the stretcher. He expected some strange alien species to be lifted out of the smaller vessel found some ten miles from the main crash site. Even his crew members were perplexed by the very human like form. There was one thing about the alien male that disturbed them even more. He was, without a doubt, beautiful.

One of his techs thought out loud as he examined the body.

"There's no blood. Maybe they're tough skinned and hard to wound."

A female tech came over and leaned in for a closer look. She used her finger to wipe something wet from a thin laceration and came away covered in a thick white liquid.

Lifting it for all to see, she said, "You are assuming they have the same blood as we do. Theirs is not red." Stunned as Professor Lancaster was, he made a note to keep her on the advanced team. She continued. "He's hurt. Very badly it seems. Hopefully our medical facilities are adequate."

Moving a lock of wet, jet black hair from the alien's pale face, she motioned for the workers to take him away.

"Well, that was surprising," another crew member spoke up.

"Yes," Professor Lancaster replied. "Yes, it was."

He motioned for them all to follow him into the makeshift lab.

The large ship could wait a bit. He knew it would take decades to figure it out but at least they had a specimen who could unlock a few doors, providing he lived.

～

Captain Darnizva found himself in a fighter ship and opened the hatch. He stared at the charred sky with patches of blue. Taking a deep breath, he choked on the air. It burned his throat for a few moments then subsided, leaving a foul taste in his mouth. Wetness on the side of his head followed by pain as he tried to sit up let confirmed it was blood. Laying back down in the cockpit he recalled the last memory, assaulting him in full force, of his second in command dragging his half-conscious body to the launch dock and strapping him into the fighter. Clearly his crew had no faith in surviving the crash but made sure at least he did.

He slammed his fist on the console, regretting the move when a searing sting spread in his hand. Something stirred off in the distance and he became alert, ignoring any pain. There was no guarantee the inhabitants of this planet were not hostile so had to make a quick decision. Standing up, he removed his cloak, sash and weapons, tossing them in the cockpit. He got out of the fighter to test the ground and liked the slight give, revealing its ability to conform.

He lifted the detachable control module for the fighter out of its console. Resembling a round edged glass slate etched with fluorescent characters, it glinted in the muted sunlight. One touch to a symbol on the right signaled rotary blades to fan out around the vessel. Another character on the tablet activated the blades and sealed the hatch. He watched as the blades tore into the dirt, forming a crater the fighter sank down into. When he deemed it deep enough, the blades were retracted. The funneled dirt collapsed on top, concealing the vessel as if nothing had been there. For good measure, he ran the tip of his boot along where the edges would be.

Far up ahead, tall structures loomed and he detected sounds that mimicked speech. A sense of despair filled the air and he knew it was because of his fleet's crash. He headed towards the area to observe the planet's species and see if he would be able to fit in. Sliding a finger on the cylindrical part of the console, the panel retracted into it. He then stored it in one of his boots.

A loud gong resounded in the air and he looked up to see a strange building with points atop it and a circle with characters around its inner perimeter. He was certain that is where the sound came from. Intrigued, he carried on and not a moment too soon for he could sense ill will approaching the area where he had landed.

Through the chaos he traveled for nearly two hours watching, listening; studying. He noticed their clothing was not much different from what he was wearing, so relaxed internally. At a clearing, he pulled out the cylinder console to check the dialect converter that was running and appeared to have deciphered the language. Tiny probes slithered out of the cylinder and into his ears. He listened to every syllable and softly mimicked the not so easy language. From what he heard, the sector he landed in was called England. Nearing the crowded streets of London, Captain Darnizva slowed his pace and watched the humans running around in a panic.

"Hey, you should bugger off!" A man running out of the large building behind him shouted. "All kinds of hell is breaking loose around us!"

"I don't think we're in any danger," Darnizva replied.

"Hmph! You're one of them brave souls think nothing

can touch ya', huh?" The man readjusted his bulky satchel and hurried off into the street. He turned back one last time gesturing towards the building. "You're just as crazy as those kids still in the dorm!"

Captain Darnizva waited for the man to go out of sight and proceeded into the building. His footsteps echoed in the empty hallways while he strolled, fascinated with the display cases along the walls. On the furthest wing, he found a room of shelves filled with variations of square objects. He extracted one of them and it splayed open. Seeing the human's language in written form, he brought out the cylinder for it to scan and decipher by matching the phonetics with the words. Three hours later, he had already read over one hundred and twenty books.

"There's still some people here!"

A young man in the hallway outside the room exclaimed, pointing to the Captain. Three other young men came into view and stopped next to him.

"Not gonna' let a little thing like the end of the world spoil your day, right?" The young man asked him.

"No. It's not the end of the world," Darnizva replied.

"Well, as long as we get out of school, I don't care," the tallest of the four said.

"He's one of them bookworms. Check it out."

The dark haired nodded his head towards the pile of books scattered on the floor.

"Why not," the tall one stated. "We got all the time in the world right now."

"Yeah, until they find out it's not the end of the world, like he said."

"What's your name?" The fourth and quietest one asked.

Captain Darnizva thought for a moment and based on the human language he answered.

"David."

"Well, David, nice to meet you. Wanna' join us?"

"Where are you going?"

"Anywhere but here, man," The dark haired one replied as he went ahead towards the exit.

Darnizva got up and walked over to the others. The tallest one stared up at him in awe. He had noticed when travelling through the city that his height was well above average.

"I'm six three, you must be at least six foot eight!"

"I never really thought about that."

The quiet one extended a hand.

"I'm Jacob." From his readings, Darnizva knew to grasp it firmly. "These two are my mates."

"Craig," the tall one said while extending his hand for a shake.

"Harry." The one who saw him first did the same.

"The one all bonkers is Fitz," Jacob explained.

Darnizva made a mental note of all their names. As much as he would love to read more of the literature in the room, a more direct approach to observing the humans through interaction was best. Stepping into the hallway, he brushed book dust from his legs and said, "I will follow you."

Fitz had come back to see what was taking them so long.

"Cool! Let's go find some desperate chicks looking for a last row." He had a huge grin on his face. "It may or may not being the end of the world and all."

A SLIGHT ARC

"I believe we may have a serious problem," Professor Makoto began.

After five years of research and containment it was now clear that some of the aliens who came down in the smaller vessels were alive and well; mating with humans. No trace of their vessels was ever found but that did not concern the scientists or their governments for that matter. Hybrid species of unknown origin was not to be tolerated unless under strict guidelines.

"We were able to quarantine nearly seventy percent of the offspring and informed the mothers that the infants had expired due to a rare disease discovered after the meteor shower. Now, we have to figure out what to do with them." Professor Headland proclaimed, tapping a pen on her notepad.

"I have a suggestion," Professor Pretchov piped in. All eyes averted on him. "We should build a facility to house and study them. Somewhere remote but still near enough to society so we can come and go without suspicion."

Professor Morandi jumped in.

"Yes, but we also need to set up some sort of program for intake. If a mother suspects she may have given birth to an infected child, they can bring them in

16

without penalty. Maybe set up a fund for the child just in case they are wrong."

"Are you suggesting we take on babies and just keep them locked in this 'facility' indefinitely?" Professor Makoto was incredulous.

"I think that is the best course of action." Professor Pretchov uncrossed his legs and sat wide in his chair as he leaned forward. "Does it not bother you that they have assimilated into our way of life in such a short time? How did they cross the language barrier? How could they blend in and act normal according to their environment? We have no idea what these hybrid children are capable of."

A long deep silence ensued as they all contemplated the input from each other and then Professor Morandi cleared her throat. She had their attention as she scanned the monitors.

"All in favor of a research facility for these new evolved humans, say aye."

"Aye!" All the scientists replied in unison.

"So, Professor Pretchov, what location did you have in mind?"

"Locations," the Professor corrected her. "We can't have just one, now can we?"

CHAPTER TWO

THE FACTORY

Involuntary Infiltration

Reporters were known to be sneaky, skeevy and prone to getting their asses caught in questionable situations. Robyn Laughlin was no exception. His camera clicked as he took pictures of his surroundings on the deserted street. Up ahead puffs of white emitted from the smoke stacks of the behemoth steel mill. After researching the plant, he found it had been decommissioned ten years ago so it was quite bizarre to see it still functioning. It was part of a story he was working on to expose government conspiracies.

The red flags showed up in the form of registered children going missing. Not in the normal sense though. There was evidence of them having been part of society's census and then nothing. Poof. Further investigation found a link to a secret government program. He had called in a few favors and burned some bridges over that information. Putting the lens cap back on, he straightened his blazer and ran his fingers through his hair.

He knew it was a big risk to go up against the government but his sense of justice would not be ignored. Over the course of two months he staked out the area, writing down the times for every vehicle along with make and model. Four vehicles made regular journeys in and out of the community. Two vans, a bulletproof tinted sedan, and a large moving truck. The 'residents' were middle class adults who rarely came home and didn't venture out when they were. No children present smacked of something unnatural.

Today was his time to move. Wrapping the camera in his jacket, he stashed it in a crack he made a week ago in an alley on the side of an old stone building. The only thing valuable on him was his identification card. The weather was fair so he wouldn't get cold on the way to the plant. Instead of loafers he had opted for sneakers in case he needed to make a run for it.

Right on schedule, the truck came barreling down the barren street towards the mill. Tapping the toe of one shoe on the ground, he jogged down, staying close to the buildings. A technique he learned from watching too many spy shows. He found it almost silly until he reminded himself of why this was important. To his surprise, the road led to a gate not standard for the plant. The modification appeared to be fairly new, towering fifty feet with solid metal enclosures to block prying eyes.

When the truck stopped at the gate, he did the unthinkable by sliding under the carriage and holding on. If it worked in the movies, why not in real life? As it moved forward, Robyn found it not so easy. His hands shook with the vibrations and he almost lost his grip. The ride seemed like an eternity. Finally, much to his relief, it came to a standstill. He watched the legs of the driver and passenger walk around to the truck's rear. Its doors rolled up and a ramp slammed down. Even straining his eyes, he couldn't see what they unloaded.

What he did notice was a space between two cargo crates wide enough to accommodate him if he squeezed in tight. It was set down in line with the rest of the load while the two men opened the loading dock. He took that chance to get into the crevice, making himself as small as possible so he wouldn't be noticed. A forklift came into view and lifted each load, carrying them in. When it came his turn, he braced himself. The trip was jarring but better than under the truck.

Inside the loading dock was dim lighting with a dinginess about the place. Each load was positioned against a wall and the two men left, securing the dock doors.

The large warehouse was immediately engulfed in darkness as the overhead lights switched off. Thankful for the cover of dark, Robyn eased from the tiny space to readjust his body. In that short instance, every muscle ached. Dust swirled around getting into his nose, forcing him to sneeze. He clamped both hands over his face to stifle the noise. From above, the afternoon sunlight struggled to pierce coated crank windows lining the edges. The effect was small thin beams of light made of swirling debris.

Robyn let his eyes adjust before heading down the main aisle, hugging the end of each row as he went. It was eerily quiet, like being in a giant tomb. He peeked at some of the inventory stacked along the aisle and noticed they were actual materials for making steel parts. At the end of his path were large clear plastic vertical blinds. Muted light emitted from the other side but as he crossed over, he found it was misleading. The new room was just as dimly lit as the warehouse before.

He stood on a walkway with metal railings and looking over saw he was a good three levels above the main. Realizing this, he crouched down and crept along the walkway, his shoes not getting much grip on the slick floor. It seemed to be coated with some sort of powder. The scent of metal permeated the air. Closer to the end were a set of stairs that took him to the next level down, where heat mixed with the coolness.

MAQUEL A. JACOB

Another level down, he glanced at the huge canisters connected by piping and the steam rising above some distance away. Not paying attention, his footing slipped. He skidded on his butt down the last ramp. For the first time, he saw people moving around. And that's when a sharp blow to the back of his head sent him reeling face down onto the floor. He saw the people's blank stares as they looked up at him before he lost consciousness.

His body felt like a ton of lead and wouldn't move. A strange tingling sensation assaulted him followed by cotton mouth. With great difficulty, he forced open his eyelids, like a thick seal broken after being glued shut. They hurt so bad he almost closed them again. More muted light stung as he tried to bring his surroundings into focus. One thing he knew was that he lay strapped down on a metal slab. An intravenous drip attached to his forearm hung from the stand by his side.

Aww fuck it all!

He chastised himself. This was not part of the plan.

He figured that if caught for any reason, whoever ran the joint would try to ruin his life on the outside or silence him on publishing the story. That was the usual cycle whenever he dove too far into government dirt. Dread filled him with the realization that he may have stumbled onto a story no one was supposed to ever hear about. He'd been roughed up a few times and even jailed, but nothing like the predicament he was in now.

Off to his left, the door opened and a man's silhouette stood in the light. Two other figures moved in one each side behind him. Robyn tensed. No mistaking the three figures attire. Robyn had been to many hospitals and could pick out a doctor or nurse. A quick sideward glance at the IV told him they were professionals. He squinted his eyes to get a better look as the trio came towards him.

The one on the right was a female nurse holding a clipboard and on the left, was another with a small, white, plastic container. Walking in between them was the male doctor, his face devoid of any well-meaning. All business. He stopped at the side of Robyn's hospital bed and stared down at him with disinterest. In one hand, the doctor held his identification card as if it were diseased.

"A reporter," the doctor said. He let out a snort and pocketed the card. "I ran your background while you were knocked out. You like to go in solo to get the story so no one can steal or beat you to it."

Already sounding ominous, Robyn braced himself for the rest of what the doctor had to say. For the first time, he cursed himself for being an ass and telling his associates to step off his turf.

"Too bad for you. The lot of you are alike. Never bothering to make actual friends. Just connections to advance your own agendas. No one will miss you."

The doctor nodded towards the drip bag and the nurse with the container opened it. She took out a syringe and stuck the needle into the small nodule. A green liquid was emptied into his drip and he began to panic which did him no good.

His body instantly went rigid and his insides burned like they were being cleaned out with a scrub brush covered in razors. Fluid and foam bubbled up his esophagus, shooting out of his mouth like a geyser. He could smell and taste chemical as his eyes rolled back.

"You should really try to get some rest," the doctor chided.

You son of a bitch! You son of a bitch! You mothefucker!
Robyn screamed at him in his head.

Convulsions wracked his body. Then, a sense of euphoria took hold. Every muscle went slack and his vision faded until total darkness consumed him. Before losing consciousness, he heard the trio's footsteps trail off as they left the room.

"Haaarrr!"

Robyn woke up trying to scream for help but it came out wrong and on top of that, hurt like hell. His throat was raw and dry as a desert. He bolted upright, clawing for the ceiling. Placing his hands over his face, he leaned over and tried to regulate his breathing. His body shook from trauma and he realized his nervous system was shot all to hell. It took a while to notice that he was not strapped down any more and wearing a hospital gown.

Of course not. I couldn't run if I tried right now.

"That's correct," a young male voice replied.

Robyn looked up, startled and afraid, and found himself face to face with a smiling young man.

"I didn't…" Robyn went wide eyed.

"No, you didn't. Not out loud anyway." The young man came around to his side and inspected him. Each touch sent pins and needles through him. "I'm a telepath. The doctor sent me in here to watch over you while you slept so I can ascertain your state of mind." He emphasized the word ascertain with a snobbish air. Finished with his task, he let out a small laugh. "You're a real idiot."

"You can go fuck yourself. When I get out of here, I will expose whatever the hell this place is."

"And that's why you're a moron," the young man laughed. "You sniffed out something not quite right and dove in without so much as a clue. You're not getting out of here."

"Watch me!"

"Your apartment has been emptied out, your last month's rent paid and a resignation notice sent to your employer."

Robyn's bowels gurgled from his immediate shock and he became woozy.

"You're lying," he whispered.

"Nope. This is a top-secret government installation. Congratulations. You found a great conspiracy. Too bad no one will know about it."

Bile rose and a stream of hateful vomit projected from his mouth. It made his shaking worse. Exhausted from the sheer power of it, Robyn fell back onto the bed. He tried to squeeze back the tears flowing down the corners of his eyes.

"Don't worry, no one's going to kill you. This will just be your new home."

The door opened and the nurse from earlier came in holding another syringe. This time, his bowels loosened and hot thick matter oozed from his anus. Knowing this, he dismissed it in lieu of anxiety from that needle. In his mind, that was far worse than having shit himself.

"Shh," the nurse cooed. She patted him on the arm and inserted the needle into the drip bag. "The doctor was being quite mean before. This is a sedative. You need to rest so you can recuperate."

It took effect on contact into his bloodstream and he drifted off.

"Someone has to clean him up. He shit himself." He heard the young man tell the nurse.

Asshole.

Sweet nothingness embraced him.

〜

Lavender scent wafted in his nostrils making his nose twitch. Hesitant to open his eyes, he laid on the bed hoping it was all just a dream.

"Nope." The young man's voice cut into his moment of peace.

Taking a deep breath and exhaling slowly, Robyn opened his eyes. He was in a different room, no less bright, and now wore a dark grey jumpsuit.

"You slept for like two days. Which may have been a good thing since the medical team came in and did the whole intake procedure."

"What is this place?"

His mouth was even drier than before. A Styrofoam cup was shoved under his face. The young man grinned. As he took the cup, his hands shook a bit causing the water to slosh around. The overhead light flickered and he glanced up in fear. He had no idea why he reacted that way. Glancing at the young man he waited for him to make his assessment.

The young man stared back at him, puzzled, then his eyes lit up.

"Oh! Hey, now. I don't dive into every single thought in someone's mind. That would be rude." Sighing, he stood up. "Hurry and drink that. We have to go. By the way, my name is Alex."

Robyn set the empty cup on the side table and swung his legs off the bed. The moment he set his weight on them, they buckled and he went tumbling forward. Alex caught him, steadying him upright. The strength in those arms amazed Robyn since the guy looked like a high schooler.

"Yep, if I had gone to school I would probably be a senior by now."

He gave Alex a frown. The selective mind reading had better stop soon.

"Sorry. Hey, can you walk alright?"

"Sure. I'll be fine. Lead the way to," Robyn waved a hand towards the door, "wherever."

Out in the corridor, Robyn sensed multiple sets of eyes on him and a buzzing in his head. It ceased seconds later leaving a blank in his mind. Alex smirked.

"Nosy people."

With that, they headed to the end of the hall where thick double doors waited for them.

Assembly Lines

Harsh metallic smells and subdued lighting greeted them as Alex pushed the doors open to reveal a fully functioning factory. Machines ran continuous products while workers did prep work. Those mechanical sounds were all he heard. And that was the eerie part. The workers were silent, even when moving around. No one spoke. He caught a glimpse of one guy bent over a press, eyes void of emotion. Like an automaton.

The place was more massive than he had first thought. Cramped rows of conveyor belts surrounded by equipment twice the size of refrigerators lined both sides of the corridor. Each one occupied by men and young boys manning the assembly lines. Not a smile amongst them. Robyn noticed the emptiness in their eyes. As if their souls had been harvested eons ago. Even a boy who appeared to be all of twelve years old.

The shock of it made him rear back and he stopped walking. Alex also halted and turned around with an inquisitive look. Robyn scanned the area, not sure what he was trying to find. Alex frowned. A sense of dread and danger welled up inside of him. He turned his attention to the people around him and found everyone staring. The glowing red exit above the door ahead beckoned.

Alex stepped closer to him, baring teeth.

"Just so you know. I am not the only telepath here so stop looking for a way out. It will get you hurt." Their eyes locked. "Keep your thoughts in check."

Robyn's eyes widened to the point where they began to sting. Alex pivoted away and continued walking. He obediently followed. They came to the end of an assembly line operated by six people, three on each side. Alex gestured with one hand towards the left. Robyn made his way to the empty section. It was so narrow that he had to go in sideways.

When he arrived at his destination, he carefully stepped over the bench and sat down. The conveyor belt ran behind, its rackety rattle in tune with the other equipment's mechanical song. Alex sat on the other side at the end directly across from the guy next to him. No one acknowledged their presence, making Robyn feel awkward. In front of him sat a young man with long, dark blonde hair. His hands were palms up relaxed on top of each other and his eyes were downcast on the work bench.

Movement caught Robyn's attention and he stared in astonishment watching the metal parts before him float upwards. They began to assemble with slow precision. He glanced at the man and for the first time, realized he was not just sitting akimbo but also floating above the bench seat. Their eyes met, startling Robyn. The parts continued coming together. Eyes void of emotion bore into him, shredding apart all his hopes and dreams. He sat frozen after the man lowered his gaze, back to the task at hand.

Feeling curiosity claw at him, Robyn turned his head to scan the rest of the row. Everyone on his side were taking parts off the conveyor belts and setting them on the work bench. On the other side, parts levitated while being manipulated by unseen forces. Many of the other assemblers had scrunched up faces, working hard at concentration. A stark contrast to the one sitting across from him.

"Don't speak!"

Alex's voice screeched in his head, causing pain.

He grabbed hold of it on instinct.

"Sorry."

This time it was a whisper. Robyn only nodded, the ringing in his head subsiding.

"We are only allowed to speak between job orders."

Blood dripped from Robyn's nose and he wiped it away as fast as he could, hearing hard soles clack against the vinyl flooring. When they stopped, he glanced down to the end of the work area and sure enough, three people stood looking at them. One was the nurse he saw when he first arrived. She gave him a haughty look that had him want to smack it off. Then she smiled.

Shit! He yelled to himself silently.

Alex shook his head, relaying his thoughts.

"No, she's not one. Any idiot can tell what you're thinking with that face."

The trio walked away at the sound of a loud klaxon. Conveyor belts squealed to a halt. Pistons clanked one last time. Machines hissed in anger at the suddenly shut down.

"You have one hour to complete your work. The new order will load when the last is assembled."

The voice in the overhead com was rough. Robyn imagined some burly red neck who would shoot first and ask questions later.

"Now we can talk," Alex said out loud.

Robyn noticed the look from Alex anticipating some form of speech but there were too many questions swirling around in his mind. Instead, he just sat motionless and silent. The metal pieces stopped in midair, causing Robyn to sit back fearful of what may come. As he did, his gaze again fell on the man across from him.

"Don't ask those things. It serves no purpose."

His voice was a soft tenor yet tinged with strength. Before Robyn could speak, the others on the line turned to him. They went in order introducing themselves, the one sitting on the far end going first.

"Chuck. I'm just an operator." He patted the side of a huge machine Robyn noticed earlier. "My assembler is Javier." Javier only nodded and continued finishing up the part floating in front of him.

"I'm Steve," the guy next to Chuck blurted out. "You better get your shit together fast. I won't let you fuck up our line." The others gave him a dirty look. "Craig needs to be able to concentrate." Indeed, his assembler had not paid any attention to them as he finished his work. Face still scrunched up in frustration, his eyes were laser focused on it. "Understand?"

"Yeah, sure. I got it." Robyn couldn't stop himself from thinking, prick.

Alex laughed out loud then clamped his hands over his mouth, fearfully looking around. When nothing happened, he uncovered his mouth and sighed.

"Yes, he is." He pointed to the man across from him. "My loader is Paul."

Turning to his right to say hello, Robyn was struck cold by the way Paul stared at the assemblers. Such disgust etched into his expression that one could feel it. At least, Robyn did.

Now aware what his role and the man across from him was, he severed his gaze from Paul and turned to his assembler.

"Donnie," the man finally said.

"Nice to meet you."

His line crew all gave him a cynical look and he realized he couldn't pull the wool over this group of people. He opened his mouth to speak and was cut off by a loud buzzer screeching through the PA speakers.

"New order will load in fifteen minutes. Set timers."

Robyn blinked a few times and down the line he saw the assembled parts were in fact gone, the workstation clear. Chuck pushed some buttons on the machine at the end and Robyn realized it ran the conveyor belt. The parts came out from it.

"What is this place?"

"A steel plant," Paul snapped.

"I know that genius," Robyn retorted. "Obviously, there's something else going on. Plus, this place was decommissioned as a functioning plant years ago."

Chuck sent him a warning stare and shook his head. The others seemed confused by his revelation then it clicked. He tried to refrain from thinking the obvious but it wasn't easy.

They have no idea about the outside.

Three hours of trying to keep up with the line's pace finally ended for Robyn at the sound of the whistles followed by equipment shutting down. He was mentally exhausted which manifested physically as well. A man in overalls came to their line with a clipboard in hand, not bothering to look up when he addressed them.

"Line 24. Your assembly met QC standards. You're free to go for the day."

He walked off and went down to the next line.

Getting up from the work bench, needle like pain spread through Robyn's legs. He faltered and fell into Paul who pushed him back roughly. An unseen wall stopped him from falling backwards. In his mind, he sensed Donnie.

"That's not necessary," Chuck chided Paul.

As they stood in the walkway near their line, Steve came up to him.

"Not too bad, but you gotta' do better than that. If we get flagged, I'm kicking your ass."

"Flagged?" Robyn was confused.

Alex grabbed him by the arm and pulled him along. Halfway down he noticed movement out of the corner of his eye. In a dimly lit hall on the opposite side, two workers were being yelled at by two higher ups. The male manager had an assembled part in his hand that wasn't quite right. It appeared mangled even though the thing held together. He shook it in front of the smaller of the workers then the other manager grabbed him by the head and smashed it into the wall. The sound made Robyn flinch, stopping him dead in his tracks. The other worker was held against the wall preventing him from interfering, anger and fear written all over in his body language. Blood pooled on the floor.

A hard shove from behind broke Robyn from the scene and when he turned to see who it was, Craig pushed him again.

"Keep moving."

"What the hell?" Robyn didn't finish.

"They got flagged," Chuck said.

His group continued down the corridor towards a large lift that already had at least twelve people on it and could accommodate more. They stepped on and the guy next to him pushed the top button of the three. There was silence the whole way. Everyone stood staring up into the ceiling except Robyn. He had his eye on the doors, getting ready for whatever came next.

The lift doors opened to a gloomy floor reminiscent of those haunted houses in horror movies. As they stepped off, lights clicked on and Robyn could see it was a recreation room. Tables with jigsaw puzzles, playing cards and board games were scattered about. A pool table sat in the far corner and three dart boards were catty corner.

Straight ahead of them was a long hallway and it too had motion lights. Some of the others went into doors along it but his crew kept going and rounded the corner.

At the second turn, they all stopped in front of a grey metal door.

"Welcome to your new home," Alex said. His smile was disingenuous.

"We have an hour to clean up and get dressed before supper," Chuck announced.

Robyn's stomach erupted into a great growl. Embarrassed, he turned away from them.

The lights switched on and the sparseness of the dorm room was made visible. His first thought was the place would have done better making barracks.

"That's what they used to be but the director felt it didn't convey enough closeness. Hence the sardine can that can hold eight of us 'comfortably.'" Alex winked as he said that last word.

Everyone began stripping off their dingy clothes covered in residue and grabbing towels from the drawers beneath their beds. Robyn went to the bare bed next to Craig's and fell onto it. His eyes were nearly closed when Alex yanked him up and shoved a towel against his chest.

"No rest for the wicked. We have to get this crap off us quick."

"What stuff," Robyn asked groggily.

"What do you think they use to manufacture steel parts?"

"I don't know, exactly."

"And you don't want to. It's nasty stuff and will cause a lot of problems."

In the bathroom were four sinks, two toilet stalls, four urinals and a massive shower stall with twelve jet heads along its walls. Steve turned the water on and steam filled the room. The moment Robyn stepped in, the force of the jets made him think his skin was being scoured off. Chuck tossed him a bottle and he fumbled to squeeze out the contents.

A thick grainy soap splooged onto his hand. It was enough to rub all over his body and it felt like scrubbing with steel wool. His skin was bright red from the water, soap combination. Another bottle was tossed at him from the other direction and he saw it was shampoo.

"What, no conditioner?" He managed a small laugh.

"Not today," Steve answered.

The shower wasn't invigorating at all, his body feeling even more tired. His stomach rumbled again and he cursed it for needing sustenance. Falling back on his unmade bed in only a towel, he closed his eyes again. Drifting off he heard the others argue.

"Leave him be."

"We have to be at the chow hall in forty minutes."

"I'll wake him up in twenty minutes."

"Just let him rest. He's an outsider. He's not like us."

Donnie crept into his head.

Don't worry. It's alright. Sleep.

So, he did.

"Come on, princess."

Alex's voice grated in his ears as he was shaken awake. He opened his eyes to Alex grinning widely mere inches from his face. Sitting up he found himself dressed in clean clothes. Grey pants. white t-shirt and a grey button down undone. He even had on socks and shoes.

"Really? You could have just woke me up. I can dress myself, you know."

"Yeah, well. You needed a nap and there was no time to wait for you to get your ass in gear."

Robyn swung his legs over the bed and immediately got nauseous. He fought the urge to retch, the tightness in his chest and esophagus intensifying. Saliva built up, filling his mouth and he drooled before the onslaught came. A bucket appeared below just in time. Another round of chemical vomit came spewing out of him and this one hurt worse. Tears stung his eyes as he gritted his teeth to lessen the impact.

"Breathe!" Chuck ordered.

He tried but more vomit came out instead.

"We don't have time for this!" Paul yelled.

"Shut up!" Alex held him tight by the underarms.

"We're going to get dinged if we're late," Paul said. His eyes burned with anger.

Their door opened and even though Robyn could only see the legs, he knew who had entered. Looking up, he confirmed it was the sadistic doctor and his equally deranged nurse. They advanced towards him with purpose, the nurse already producing a needle and pushing out a squirt of liquid from the syringe.

"Wait! Stop!" Alex cried.

He was yanked to the side and the nurse was on Robyn in seconds, jamming the needle into his abdomen. She pinned him down flat and pushed down on the plunger. Her smile was the evilest thing he had ever seen.

"I had a feeling he may not feel too swift after working in the plant for so long so soon." The doctor gave a tight-lipped grin. "He'll be fine in about five minutes. Plenty of time to get to the hall."

The nurse yanked out the needle and got up. She followed the doctor out, turning to give him a wink before disappearing into the corridor.

"Those fuckers!" Steve spat.

"Are you okay?" Alex's voice expressed hurt.

Robyn wiped his mouth and sat up. All he could do was nod. The nausea was in fact subsiding quickly and he could breathe normally again.

"We have to go," Paul reiterated.

Chuck grabbed him by the front of his shirt and

slammed him into the wall.

"We know that! He's part of our crew now, so cut it out."

The thought of food was no longer appealing to Robyn but his stomach once again gave protest after being completely emptied.

Chow hall etiquette resembled prison protocol. Single file line, one crew at a time, no talking except to ask the kitchen helper what you wanted. Although the food actually looked appetizing, Robyn could tell there was a lot of protein and supplement based food stuff. He had seen plenty from his ex-girlfriend who had been on the whole organic health kick. Much of what he remembered was on either end of the taste spectrum; Either bland or outright nasty, never in-between. They got their meal and went to an empty table.

Robyn scanned the massive hall, seeing that the number of workers and staff filled less than a third of its space. A familiar face caught his eye and he zeroed in on the line worker from earlier. His head was bandaged, part of it covering one eye. The left arm was in a sling and he could make out his torso wrapped in Ace bandage. His hands shook as he used a spoon to lift his food into his mouth. The other worker who had been with him in the hall sat across from him, fuming from an internal fight he seemed not to be winning.

The wounded worker halted his spoon midway and locked eyes with Robyn. So much pain and suffering emitted immobilized him. He could see how young the worker was and a fire of rage lit inside of him.

S'okay, he heard the soft whisper of the worker.

His partner's eyes went wide, his head snapping up and he turned around towards Robyn.

"Don't stare," Alex said.

That broke his concentration and he watched the worker resume eating.

"This is wrong."

"Shh."

"All of it."

Robyn put a hand on his forehead and bent down to eat, not letting anyone see the tears well up. Chuck, sitting next to him, patted him on the back. None of the them spoke the rest of the meal. All he could think about now was not getting flagged and had no idea how to prevent such a thing. A flash of Alex came to him.

Latent Powers

Deciding to bide his time, Robyn did what he was told and tried not to cause any ripples while working. Once a week, the workers were allowed a day off to relax in the rec room or visit with other workers on the dorm floor. It was done on rotation since the plant ran seven days a week. Whenever he could, he 'got lost' to find out more information about the place. With the new technique Alex had taught him on how to censor his thoughts, not many knew his motives. As far as others were concerned, he had been defeated into his fate.

Not on your life! I'm getting the fuck out of here to expose these monsters.

Today, he ventured far into the lab sector where a few offices were. Six months had already gone by and he knew his excuse of being new was on the verge of wearing out. He was sure the director understood his movements and dismissed it as desperation. But, Robyn was underestimated a lot in his profession and the director had no idea how resourceful he could be.

The labs were too secure for him to get into without an inside man. He found out many of the files were stored elsewhere in the sector and it lay beyond the offices. Overhead cameras lined the hall leading to it so he waited for the weekly haul of records. Squeaky wheels came down the corridor of the hallway where he hid.

Right on time, the worker stopped in front of the lab doors and parked the two-tiered rolling bin. The moment he went in, Robyn hurriedly rearranged the bottom shelf and squeezed himself in. His body was leaner from the lack of real food and stress so he folded nicely. He heard the click of the lab door open then close and extra weight came down on him from more files were dumped on top. The cart began moving down to the filing room.

Once inside, the cart was shoved up against a shelf while the worker wrote in a log book. Robyn wiggled out of his tight hideout and into another small part of the shelf, moving a few file boxes around him for good measure. The worker went to task of filing the documents in swift order as if he wanted to be finished quickly. Some of them, Robyn noticed, he filed wrong. When he was done and left, Robyn slid out.

He had fifteen minutes, twenty tops, before the man came back for his second drop off and a reload for the file requests from the labs on the other side. They did this to reduce access and not have files all over the place which he thought was a smart move. After a few minutes of reading the cabinet labels, his attention fell on one that said Bi-Genetic Research. Flipping through the drawer he pulled out one about analysis.

A few keywords stood out as he read and at first, he couldn't fathom any of it being true. As he read on, his mind nearly overloaded.

Alien DNA...gender shifts.... talent markers.... experiments.

All the documents pertaining to those made him ill to the core. This was not just some steel mill being used for government secrets. It was a prison for children with alien elements. Cut off from the world and treated as lab rats for scientific gains. The fact that he could read all of those and retain it was contributed to the concoction he was injected with in the beginning. According to the documents, the government was introducing alien DNA into humans to see if they could create super soldiers. Each person manifested different traits. This level of speed reading combined with photographic memory was his and he wasn't sure if he liked it.

So engrossed in the docs, Robyn nearly jumped out of his skin when he heard the cart wheels squealing outside the door. Shoving the file back in the drawer, he returned to his hiding place and waited for the cart. His heart rate was elevated and he could hear himself breathing loudly. Taking a deep breath, he exhaled slowly and calmed himself. By the time the worker came back, he had made himself silent as the dawn.

There was a little less on the bottom after the worker unloaded then reloaded but Robyn managed to arrange them around so not to be seen. As the cart stopped near another lab, he carefully slithered out and pushed the files back in nice and neat. Breathing out heavily, he slid up the wall to stand and made his way back to the stairwell. He struggled to keep a lid on his thoughts all the way to the dorm.

Inside, he found his mates lounging on their beds instead of mingling with the other workers in the recreation room. Alex gave him a quizzical look before going back to the book he was reading. Donnie stared at him knowingly and he almost panicked. Remaining calm, he went to lay down. His heart beat was racing and he placed a hand on his chest, feeling the hard thumps.

All the information swirling in his mind unleashed and he couldn't stop it. He noticed Alex, Donnie, and

Craig invade, making him sit up in fear. His gaze fell on them as their eyes went wide. Then a black out in his mind. Alex had forced a curtain inside.

"Where did you find all that?" Alex hissed in anger and terror.

"Don't," Donnie said.

Craig came to sit by him and grabbed his head with both hands. His face was contorted in a state of confusion and…hate. But not for him.

"You cannot make any of that known. Do you understand?"

Robyn nodded, the expression on Craig's face making him want to run from the room.

"What's going on?" Paul demanded. "What the fuck has he done, now?" Paul came at him, trying to pry Craig away. "I'll fucking kill you if we get caught up in your shit!"

"Enough!"

Chuck pulled him away and even Craig let him go. The tension in the room thickened.

The main door burst open and the good doctor stood in the hall. He was visibly irritated as his gaze bore into Robyn. The corners of his mouth twitched upwards until a forced smile formed.

"Robyn! I was so worried about you since it seemed you had gotten lost. Again."

"I can't seem to get my bearings, you know. This place is so damn big."

Robyn scratched his head in mock embarrassment. He too gave a false smile.

"Well, let's remedy that. Your crew will be working maintenance for the next thirty days." His roommates collectively sucked in their breaths. "So, your movements are limited to the factory floor and these barracks."

A real smile spread across his face.

"I'm sure you'll learn a lot in that time."

The doctor slammed the door shut and Paul took a flying leap at Robyn. Both men fell tumbling to the floor, Robyn's arms in front of him in an X to block Paul's relentless blows. Once Chuck got a hold of him and pulled him off, Robyn could see the defeated looks on the others faces. Donnie was more cold than usual.

"I…"

Alex raised a hand to stop him from saying any more.

"Maintenance means we get to watch Donnie go into the core of one the boilers for repairs and hope he comes out alright. If things go hinky, we have to shut it down, whether he's out of it or not."

Robyn clenched his fists as he fought the sting of tears.

"No use crying now!" Paul yelled. "I knew you would screw us!"

"Shut up!" Steve and Chuck responded.

Paul went back to his bed and curled up in a ball.

"I'm a reporter. It's what I do," Robyn said deadpan.

"You really think you can get out of here," Alex said.

Donnie looked past them all at the door.

"He can. Just not right now. Time."

Wrong Place for Love

How long?

It was getting hard to keep track of time as his imprisonment went on. That brought him out of a dead sleep in the middle of the night. Robyn knew it had been well over a year, hell maybe two, and the bond between his roommates grew. It became apparent what kind of relationship Donnie and Steve were in after he caught them in the bathroom one time after lights out. He could only call the sex they were engaged in as desperate,

43

considering their environment. Steve's face expressed fervent lust mixed with anger while Donnie just took it all in defeat.

He didn't judge them, feeling a bit jealous since he opted to sneak there in the middle of the night sometimes to jack off with a rag shoved in his mouth so no one would hear. Well, one person did hear, or rather, knew about it. Alex was in his head more and more lately. And not just telepathically. Something about the young man made him disoriented; frustrated. He could literally smell him from down a hallway. The more they stayed in contact, the worse his erection became.

In the documents he had perused in the storage room, there was a passage about Bi-Genetics having a small group for compatibility and how they could detect each other that way. Having a true soul mate was great and all, but this place was not the right environment for eternal love. That said, he still found himself staring at Alex's sleeping figure on occasion. Every two months, Alex was forced to be in female form for menstruation. He got to see how well that body was maintained. Firm, taunt, athletic; young. He had forgotten how old Alex was. Was he legal? Even his chestnut brown hair had gotten longer, almost touching the area of his lower back and Robyn fought the urge daily to run his fingers through it.

A stirring caught his eye and when he located it, found Paul turned around in his bed glaring at him in the dark. The two men stayed like that while the seconds ticked by. Paul disengaged first and rolled back over. Robyn sat up on his elbows and let his head flop back against the wall. His hair had also gotten a bit long again, resting on his shoulders. A haircut was due but Alex loved it because he could wrap his fingers around the strands. Every time he did that, Robyn got a boner.

Fuck!

Aggravated, he slid down under the covers and forced himself to get some sleep.

The plant was unusually busy with massive orders coming nonstop throughout the shift. Each section was given their meals on the line with only fifteen minutes to wolf it down before resuming production. Robyn never got used to the silence of every human in the place. His eyes glanced over at Alex eating the cold cut sandwich and zeroed in on his lips ready to take a bite. Midway, Alex stopped and Robyn slammed down an iron curtain on his thoughts so he couldn't read his mind. He wasn't sure if he made it in time because Alex didn't look up or acknowledge him, continuing to eat. Across from him, Donnie's deadpan stare showed a slight twitch.

At the end of day, back in their room, Donnie yanked him aside in the farthest corner of the bathroom.

"You do know, right?" He asked bluntly.

"Yeah," Robyn replied as he snatched his arm out of Donnie's grip. "It's obvious." He gave a nod towards the bunks. "Was that what happened with you and?"

"No. It was out of..." Donnie shrugged.

"So, Alex is like click bait for me."

"They chose him for a reason and don't think for one moment they're not pissed at him for not seducing you right off the bat."

"You're talking a lot today." Robyn gave a tight-lipped smile.

"Because you know too much and will get us all in a world of hurt."

Robyn balled his hands into fists and tensed up.

"So, I'm supposed to just give them what they want?"

"Would you rather they facilitated it for you?"

"What?"

45

Robyn reared back, hitting the wall behind him.

Donnie let out a sigh and walked away leaving Robyn confused, and afraid.

He went back into the bunk area and stripped his work uniform off. The rank odor of sweat, oil and metal radiating from his armpits nearly overpowered him as he lifted his shirt over his head. Another smell mingled with it. Musky yet slightly sweet, like cream. Alex had walked past him into the bathroom. He pressed the shirt firmly down on his crotch and waited until the others were in there before moving.

While his roommates relished under the hot pressured water, he snuck in sideways so no one would notice. As he turned to push the water on, he saw Alex standing under the water next to him in a state of oblivion. Darkened by the water, his hair cascaded down his back, forming slimy tendrils due to the oil build up.

Without thinking, Robyn ran his fingers down through it, feeling each slippery strand. Alex's posture straightened and his gaze wandered over to land on his semi erection. Robyn's shower nozzle picked that moment to shoot scalding hot water down on him and he thanked the Gods as his dick went flaccid from the heat.

Dinner in the chow hall was even more quiet and the tension was thick. Robyn took a few quick glances around and realized why. Everyone was exhausted. The last few shifts had been grueling, lasting fourteen or sixteen hours as opposed to the normal ten. Whatever those orders were for must have been important. He guessed at a military contract. Who else would need such high demand in such a short time frame?

The observers patrolled the area, stopping at each table to make sure the food was being eaten. No one could leave unless every tray was empty regardless if it made you sick later. Massive calorie intake to replenish what they burned earlier. The archive files calculated it at an outrageous ten thousand a day. Despite the exhaustion, he knew some would try to get their sex on and needed the energy.

At least they cared that much.

He smirked to himself and immediately closed his mind off. Some of the telepaths were quick to pick up on it and their gaze fell on him. To his surprise, there was no malice this time. Only an acknowledgement of submission.

While the rest of the roommates went to the recreation room, Robyn and Alex stayed behind. Alex, because he was tired. Robyn had something else in mind. Donnie's words echoed in his head.

Give them what they want.

But it wasn't only about what they wanted. He couldn't stand it any longer. In the gloomy dark of the room, he crawled on to Alex's bed where he lay on his side and knelt over him. All that hair splayed across the top of the blanket covering him beckoned to be abused in Robyn's mind. Their eyes locked. He reached out and slowly gathered Alex's hair into his hand, letting it get tangled around his fingers. Alex stirred then turned over, his hair becoming more twisted in Robyn's hand.

He used his other hand to pull the covers off and exposed Alex's entire body. The thin button down and scrub like pants were pitiful obstacles to overcome. Robyn leaned down and kissed him, tentatively, wanting to know the feel of his lips. When he sat up, Alex had a look of anxiety. He kissed him again, this time with more pressure until there was a bit of resistance. Again, he disengaged to see what Alex would do. Despair. That is what he saw and it angered him. The next kiss he went full on and Alex finally responded in kind. Their tongues ran across each other and he said telepathically.

Shift.

Alex tried to halfheartedly push him off.

Don't. I'm tired.

I don't care.

Robyn gripped his hair tighter and pulled so that his face was perpendicular to the ceiling. He took hold of Alex's pants waist and yanked them off, then waited. Giving in, Alex's body began to shift. Robyn watched with fascination and impatience as Alex's average sized penis rescinded into nothingness. He wished he had a small light to shine down there to witness it fully. The swell of breasts formed, ripping open the shirt to set them free.

He let his hand roam the soft mounds before traveling down between warm, firm thighs. Now fully in female form, Alex shuddered from the light touch of his fingers as they moved playfully along. Her body arched as he slipped them inside. The heat of her womb intensified as the sticky wetness ooze between his fingers.

The smell! That musky, creamy scent was tenfold and hit sensors in his brain that sent him on the verge of borderline madness. He clumsily pulled off his pants and used his legs to open hers wider.

Don't hurt me. Alex whispered in his head.

Robyn dismissed it and plunged his aching erection deep into her. He hadn't had sex in so long, there was no way he wasn't going to be a little rough. Alex's eyes squeezed shut and she gritted her teeth so not to make a sound.

Screw that! I want to hear her.

His grip on her hair tighten until she gasped out loud. Something within him switched on and he dove deeper until there was nowhere else to go. She cried out, making his skin tingle with excitement. Locking his lips

48

with hers, he let his tongue explore as he reared back for a long, hard thrust. Her fingers dug into his bare back, her mouth opening wider. Her nails, though cut short, pierced his skin as he went for a third time. Releasing her from his savage kiss, he set a pace that he knew would leave her no rest. Her moans and cries of pain egging him on.

The Doctor stood in the doorway of the dark room and watched them with a smile on his face. They were so entwined with each other physically and psychically that his presence didn't register. He moved silently into the room and sat down in the lounge chair near the door. Crossing his legs, he sat back and waited for them to finish.

He fucks like an animal.

Which was not surprising. Granted, Robyn probably hadn't had any in a while even before he came to the mill, but judging from his personality, the Doctor had a hunch. The inadequate database they had comprised so far was nevertheless quick to kick out a viable mate for the former journalist. Alex was no virgin but had never experienced such brutality. Not while conscious.

Robyn felt the synchronicity as they brimmed towards climax. He also sense being observed but that couldn't be. Right? Alex tensed, her eyes round like saucers. Out of the corner of his vision he could see a silhouette in the chair.

Oh God!

Too late. There was no turning back. He wasn't going to stop until he had his fill and didn't give a rat's ass if they came screaming in ecstasy for his enjoyment. And they did. His free hand slammed into the wall above for leverage as he claimed the final thrust, unleashing his seed inside her. It was painful and satisfying, letting the pent-up rage ebb with its flow.

Sweat drenched, exhausted and mortified, Robyn and Alex turned to see the Doctor rise from the chair and grin down at them. His gleeful expression of accomplishment sent dread through them.

"You should get cleaned up before bed. Don't want to subject your fellow roommates to the stench of freshly done sex."

As he left out of the room, Alex let out a strangled cry and tears of horror replaced those of release. Robyn punched the wall before letting it slide down as he buried his head in her neck.

Paul leaned against the wall by the farthest toilet and watched Alex vomit violently. He folded his arms and grimaced.

"Congratulations on getting knocked up with a kid you'll never get to see," he laughed condescendingly.

"Shut up!" Robyn pushed him away. "If you're not going to help, just go."

Donnie wet a hand towel and brought it over for him. Robyn laid it against the back of Alex's neck. Another wave of vomit gushed out of him and he coughed, trying to catch his breath.

"You know what happens next, right?" Paul smirked.

"So, help me!" Robyn stood up ready to go after him but Chuck blocked his path.

"Go somewhere else, Paul," Chuck ordered.

Disgusted, Paul left the bathroom.

"This isn't what I planned," Robyn said softly.

"You gave them what they wanted," Donnie said.

"What?"

"Free, unregistered test subjects to mold how they want. There's a maternity ward and a children's area inside this monstrosity."

Robyn's eyes went wide. He rubbed Alex's back as Steve's words sunk in. He remembered seeing information about it but he figured it was at a separate location since this was a steel mill. Alex grabbed hold of the toilet bowl and pushed himself up. His legs were wobbly but managed to stand on his own.

"I'm okay now."

"But this situation isn't," Robyn snapped. He turned to Donnie. "What happens now? Do you know?"

"I do," Donnie replied sadly. He lightly touched his abdomen then let his arms hang loose. "They'll come take you a month before you're due and you don't come back for four months."

"What about…?" Robyn began to ask.

"I have no idea where they keep the children but because of our psychic connection, I know he's alright."

"How can you say that? This place? No one is alright here!"

"He's alive!" Paul stepped in to retort. "That's all we can wish for."

That made everyone go quiet. Robyn wrapped Alex in his arms and held him tight. A new vow swam to the surface of his mind and at its first inception, the others shielded his thoughts. The journalist in him resurfaced and he wasn't going to let the corruption surrounding him stand a moment longer. Timing was the key and for that, he would wait.

Hostile Takeover

An epic fight was what Robyn envisioned when they came to take Alex away. He would try to protect her while she struggled, kicking and screaming as two orderlies dragged her off. Guards would hold the others back so they couldn't interfere. The doctor, grinning with

51

pleasure at their wasted efforts, stood in the doorway for optimal view.

None of that happened.

Dim slivers of light spread across the dark room as the door opened. Two orderlies, that bitch nurse and the doctor stood in the hallway. Robyn reared up, ready for combat but was slammed back down onto the bed by the nurse. Her speed defied logic and he wondered again if she was modified like him. Even in the dark, he could see her distorted facial expression and teeth gleaming behind that sinister smirk. He tried to push her off but found her strength far exceeded his. Almost inhuman. In his side view, he saw the orderlies push a needle into Alex's neck and her body go limp.

"You didn't really think we'd harm her?" The doctor leaned against the doorframe. "She's carrying precious cargo. Fighting is not good for someone in her condition."

The orderlies gently carried Alex out of the room past the doctor. His mouth curved into the same grin he imagined in his scenario.

"You son of a …"

He noticed movement above him and turned to see the nurse's fist come down on him like a hammer on impact but didn't knock him out. After the third punch, he was sent into oblivion.

A raging headache woke him up a little before dawn. Robyn sat up slowly so not to jar himself. He held the side of his head and tried to squeeze away the pain. From across the room, Paul sat up in his bed and stared at him for a bit before laughing out loud.

"Oh, you got it good!"

Robyn narrowed his eyes in disgust and let his hand drop from his head.

"Why didn't you help me?" He yelled.

"Did you all enjoy that last night?" He added.

"Now hold on," Chuck said with a raised hand.

"Aww, you mad?" Paul snickered.

"Stop!" Donnie ordered. He swung out of his bed and came to stand over Robyn. "There was no point in fighting because the outcome would have been the same. And the doctor was right. You wouldn't have wanted Alex to fight in her condition."

Robyn punched his mattress and fought back the stinging tears threatening to flow. His vision blurred as they finally filled up. Donnie placed a hand on the top of his head.

The door flew open, causing a small breeze to flutter. Standing with utter disdain, the line lead made sure his stare focused on all of them. He raised the clipboard that never left his side and glanced at it.

"Since you're down one and you," he eyed Robyn, "are considered useless on the floor, there will be a change in duties. Steve and Robyn, you'll be working the docks and the warehouse for the next three months."

"Wait a minute," Paul interrupted. "What about Donnie? Robyn is his line helper."

"The furnace." The line lead smiled. "Don't worry. It will only be routine maintenance this time."

"Mother fu…" Paul started.

"I will not tolerate that language in my presence!" The line lead hollered. "Get your asses in gear. You start today."

As he left, Chuck let out a snort.

"Language, huh? But, if he does it, that's okay?"

"This is bullshit!"

Paul threw a pillow across the room.

"At least you'll only be doing minimal work," Robyn said to Donnie.

"You think they aren't going to force him to do

maintenance on that monstrosity?" Paul asked angrily.

The man had a point. Robyn chastised himself for not knowing any better after all this time. It was going to come to an end in three months' time. Alex's return would be his deadline. Looking up at Donnie, their eyes met and a promise flowed between them. The factory was going to have new overseers.

~

His shoulders square across the tiles, Robyn leaned back settling his full weight against the shower wall. Exhaustion spread through his whole body and he let his head rest, feeling the cold smooth ceramic on his scalp. His hair, longer with deep waves, brushed the skin just above his shoulders. Working the docks was hard labor and he imagined it must be what prison was like. The only bonus; he was pretty ripped with muscles. From the constant rotation of uniforms he went through, he figured himself twice his original size.

Alex would love this. Dark long hair, manly physique. Shit, I'm sexy as hell.

He thought about her often to keep his sanity. On occasion, they would link minds and he could see through her eyes. The first time was to let him see what their son looked like at four days old. It shook him, to the point of being inconsolable. He had never cried so much in his life. But, it also gave him resolve.

Reaching behind him, he turned on the shower and let the hot water drench him. He didn't move for a while, forgoing soap. To his right, he saw Steve slumped down on the tiled floor half asleep. Working the warehouse after the docks meant they ate dinner well after everyone else. He was starving yet too tired to make the trek to the mess hall. However, if they didn't there would be hell to pay. Conjuring up what little strength he had, Robyn grabbed the soap and cleaned off the sweat and dirt. He needed all the fuel he could get.

The doctor sensed a change in the workers' mood and began to prep for a coup. Every now and again he would catch telepathic snippets speed through the air. He wasn't sure what the end game was supposed to be. A takeover would be meaningless unless they were going to acquire the government contracts. Having a hostage plan didn't do much good either since not many could leave the factory to begin with. Regardless of the plan, he would thwart it at every level.

And he knew who started it. Ever since Robyn had come to the factory, things had changed. There was more rebellion and noncompliance on the lines. It escalated the closer to Alex's release.

At the maternity ward, he walked up to the head nurse. He took a glance behind him at the rows of hospital beds facing each other along walls. They were all occupied by heavily sedated pregnant Bi-genetics in female form. No reason for them to wander around.

"Is everything prepared?" He asked the nurse.

She seemed to fidget as she turned towards him. Uncertainty.

"Yes, it's all been," she paused. "Is this really necessary, doctor?"

He glared at her and she flinched away from him.

"Don't question my methods."

"Yes, doctor, I'm sorry."

He pivoted away from her and headed to the door. Halfway, he stopped and made note of the I.V. drips attached to the girls. Such a pity. Resuming his exit, he left the nurse to finish her duties.

⤳

Again, Robyn's prediction on how things would go was off the mark. This time he figured they were in for some fanfare with Alex being presented like a prize. No. When he came in from his last night of working at the docks, he found Alex back in male form sound asleep on his own bed. Robyn moved silently into the bathroom and shut the door, not wanting to wake everyone. Steve was already in there, failing to hold himself up any longer.

Finally clean and slightly rejuvenated, Robyn went back into the room and slid next to Alex, facing him. He noticed the roundness of his features indicating Alex still carried some baby weight. The furrowed lines on his forehead and ragged breathing were tell-tale signs of stress. He softly caressed his face. A low squeal sound emitted from Alex's lips as if he were in pain. Out of the corner of his eye, he saw Steve motioning for him. He kissed Alex on the lips and slid off the bed, careful not to shake it.

"I'll fix it, baby. I promise," he whispered in his ear.

Then he stood up and followed Steve out. The whole way, he had to dampen his rage.

Two weeks went by and the day to start their freedom had arrived. All the workers involved did their jobs as usual to alleviate suspicion but Robyn knew the good doctor smelled trouble in the air. Groups were formed to tackle different sectors and they all coordinated to implement the plan simultaneously. He wanted to make sure none of the staff could go off and give aide to others. Scanning the cafeteria during lunch break, he made eye contact with the duo from his first month in the factory. They both gave a tiny nod towards him before averting theirs.

Next to him, Alex sat slumped against the wall. His arms hung loosely at his sides as he stared into nothing.

He nudged him to sit up straight when one of the guards came strolling by on his rounds. The man gave them all a look that said, I dare you. Robyn smiled and thought, Bring it! The guard stopped. A few of the workers looked up from their meal in surprise. Donnie sent a sideways glance of caution. Finally, the guard hmphed and continued his patrol.

"What the hell are you doing?" Chuck whispered as he leaned close.

"What?" Robyn shrugged.

"Not funny," Paul hissed.

"Like they don't know."

"Then, what's the point of having a plan?" Steve asked, also whispering.

"It's not a matter of what, but how."

"That makes no sense," Paul said.

"Trust me."

"I don't." Paul stared at Donnie. "He's going to get us all killed."

"They're not going to kill us. We're too valuable," Donnie added.

The ten-minute warning sounded and everyone hurried to finish eating. This time, they really did need all the fuel for the fight to come.

Alarms went off across the factory as machines ground to a halt from the emergency stops being activated. Line workers abandoned their posts, spreading out like ants, and took down the guards at each interval. They spilled out into the main halls and headed for the offices, storage units and the docks. Robyn led his group consisting of Donnie, Paul, Alex and Steve towards the maternity ward.

Many of the office workers escaped to the labs, not realizing they had been corralled like cattle towards them. The moment they locked themselves in, the security mechanism activated. Metal shutters came down and sealed the room. Inside, the office workers and scientists panicked.

"Stay calm, people," one of the scientists yelled. The din of noise lessened to a manageable decibel. "We just need to override the system with the code." He waved a card sized laminated placard."

He had just placed it on the card reader attached to a wall panel when the power flickered and it spit forth an electrical arc. On the monitor that showed the other side of the barricade, he could see the workers cheering in triumph.

"Ahh, shit!"

"What? What just happened?" A female from the office wing asked.

"It's a safety feature. If the code isn't used then the main company is notified. This lab will be locked down until the support team arrives."

"And how long before they get here?" Another office worker snapped.

"Three days."

Yelling ensued. The scientist was accosted by a few people and his colleagues came to his rescue. Another scientist hit the intercom button on the panel and addressed the workers.

"We know you can break through this. If you open this barricade, I promise you no harm." Some of the others in the room turned and stared at him incredulously. They were not on board with it. "Look, this thing won't open for three days. Do you really want us starving to death on your conscience?"

The doctor watched the chaos unfold on his monitors in the command center. He pushed the intercom button.

"Activate the nullification shield."

That should do the trick

It was a safety feature that blocked any powers the workers may have, putting them and the guards on equal levels. He was well aware Robyn's first destination would be to rescue the children, mainly his own. In a moment of curiosity, the doctor decided to meet them there; give them a taste of helplessness. The workers may outnumber the staff but he held all the cards.

All over the plant, workers with talent grabbed hold of their heads in pain and were momentarily open for retaliation. At the lab, scientists and office personnel watched as the workers dropped to their knees. One of them recovered quicker than the others and looked up at the camera with a smirk on his face.

"Sorry, pal. We can't do anything now."

The scientist with the code card backed up against one of the metal workstations. His face contorted in pain. Then the rest of the room went silent as they figured out what just happened.

"We're screwed. Oh my god, what are we going to do?" A male office guy asked.

"We have to wait for the support team."

"For three days?" A female scientist screamed.

A dull thud, as if a heavy curtain was thrown, invaded Robyn's head. Paul staggered into a nearby barricade in the hall.

"Fuck!"

He lost his balance as he tried to hold himself up one handed, the other holding the side of his head.

"What was that?" Steve asked, shaking his head.

"What I told you about earlier. It's pretty annoying."

"You didn't hear me," Alex said.

"Hmm?"

"I was talking to you."

"Telepathically?" Alex nodded. "Yeah, I didn't. That's what just happened."

"Sons of bitches," Paul exclaimed.

"Let's keep going. We're almost there," Robyn commanded.

He had given them fair warning but unless they had experienced it beforehand, it was still a shock. Leave it to a bunch of scientists to come up with something so disgusting. They rounded the corner and continued until they came to the maternity wing's steel double doors. Robyn and Steve pushed the doors open and on the other side stood the doctor. His hands were casually in his pockets as he eyed them, obviously amused.

"Came to a fight with no way to defend yourselves. That isn't very smart."

"I think you're mistaken," Robyn replied.

"A field to block your powers has been activated."

Robyn smiled wide. "I knew you'd do that. But you forgot one thing."

"And what's that?"

"In the history of uprisings, the only weapons needed were resolve and these." Robyn held up his fists.

The doctor scoffed then removed his hands from his pants pockets.

"So be it."

Before he could move, Steve had the doctor by the throat and hauled into the hallway. The double doors swung shut, metal slamming against metal. The two nurses in the room backed away from Robyn and his group. The nearest one reached across her desk and grabbed hold of a small cylinder with a button atop it. A blinking light on the side coincided with an indicator on the computer screen. The other nurse was inching closer to the door on the far side that led to the children's ward.

"You stop this madness right now or I push this button." The first nurse stated. "This will send a poison through every I.V."

Donnie stepped towards her, his face contorted with fury.

"You would kill every Bi-Genetic and unborn child in here?"

"That's right!" The second nurse yelled. "All of those abominations will be destroyed."

"In that case." Donnie was on the second nurse in a flash, grabbing her hair to pull her down while he bent her arm back. They both went down to the ground and Donnie got close to her ear. "I'll just tear you apart for vengeance." He pulled hard, dislocating her shoulder and she screamed.

The other nurse went pale and took another step back.

"You hit that button, and you're next. They die and you follow," Paul said.

"I…" she stuttered.

"Are a murderer just like the rest of them."

"Please, stop!" She cried out to Donnie as he pulled harder until they all heard a loud cracking sound.

The second nurse's face was covered in snot and tears, her eyes nearly bulging out of their sockets. She had stopped screaming and gone into shock. Horrified, the first nurse tossed the cylinder across the room then slid down to the floor with her head in her hands. Donnie let go and the second nurse seemed to melt as her limbs relaxed. Alex went to each bed and disconnected the I.V.'s.

Paul and Donnie stepped over the second nurse and opened the far door. Inside, Donnie moved to the center of the room and looked around. Robyn noticed many of the children were either scared or drugged. This was not where the infants were kept but all the same, he was pissed.

"Esthen," Donnie called out.

None of the children moved and there was no response. A hologram of a small boy flickered into existence at the bottom of the bed near Donnie. With each flicker, the imaged solidified until it became flesh. The little boy was maybe five years old with straw hay colored hair in disarray. He wore animal print pajamas and no socks. His tiny hands gripped the rail of the bed frame.

"There you are." Donnie reached out and lifted the boy up into his arms.

"Momma," the little boy said.

Paul stood stiff with clenched fists until Donnie turned and handed him their son. Esthen caressed Paul's cheeks with both hands then gave him a kiss. Paul held him for a long time, his eyes closed tight. When they released, Esthen dropped to the floor and took his father by the hand. He pulled him towards yet another door on the opposite end. Robyn, Donnie and Alex followed.

It opened to a massive room filled with hospital cribs. A third of them were occupied by newborns, some a few months old. Alex began checking each one to find their son. Halfway through, he stopped dead in his tracks and inhaled sharply. Robyn made his way to see what was wrong and he too halted in shock.

At four months old, their son was by no means small but he had obviously lost some weight. There was a needle mark on the side of his head. Watery pink specks dotted his lips and as he coughed, more came up. His little hands shook.

"I knew," Alex cried softly.

"What?" Robyn was confused.

"I shielded you from it. I could feel he was distressed

and knew they were doing something bad to him." Alex hung his head, tears dripping down into the crib. "I knew."

To their surprise, the infant opened his eyes. As soon as he saw them, he smiled and started giggling. Pink saliva bubbles rose. Esthen climbed up and stroked his head. Robyn went around to the side of the crib and picked up his son. He wadded up the blanket and used it to wipe his face. He brought him close, smelling his son's natural scent and breathed in deep. A sense of peace and pure love engulfed him.

Loud thuds followed by crashes emitted from the maternity ward and they all turned to the open door. For the sound to travel that far meant Steve might be in trouble. With babies in tow, they all headed back to see what was happening.

The first thing they encountered was the scared nurse doing triage on the other. She gave them a hateful stare then resumed her work. Ahead was the doctor flying backwards in the air, arms and legs loosely extended before hitting the wall. He seemed in shock for a moment then moved in time as Steve charged into him, missing. Paul took up where he left off and grabbed the doctor by his shirt collar.

"You think you've won this?" The doctor wheezed.

"Not at all. But we will not be slaves for you any longer," Donnie replied.

The doctor let out a laugh. He stared down Paul until he released him. He fell back in a heap and straightened out to sit with one knee bent.

"This plant is under government contract. If production halts, you'll have all kinds of military might coming here to remedy the problem."

Still holding his son, Robyn leaned over him and bared his teeth.

"Oh, I don't think so."

"Try it," the doctor threatened.

Robyn looked around and saw worried expressions on his group's faces. He had to decide if the doctor was bluffing or not and fast.

⌇

And that's that!

Robyn sighed inwardly as he leaned against the open dock doors. No longer in the factory issued scrub work clothes, he wore full length black cargo pants and a black mock turtle neck. The rest of his group wore the same. He watched the warehouse workers coordinate with the dock personnel to get the latest shipment out on time. A negotiation was in progress between him and the head of the factory.

The doctor was correct. No sooner had the lock down ended in the office sector, a group of mercenaries came through like ninjas. All the workers were surrounded before they could figure out what was happening. One saving grace was that the head was not pleased with how the doctor had been running things. His liaison, along with the doctor, came up to them on the platform and Robyn shifted his weight to the other side.

"The great savior," the liaison greeted him.

"I don't see how, considering we are still trapped in here."

"As you should be," the doctor said.

Robyn's eyes narrowed and Alex gently caressed his arm.

"This factory is part of a bigger wheel. You saw some of the work being done and the files collected. The public cannot know of such things."

"They deserve to know all of it!" Robyn snapped. "It impacts humanity itself."

"All in due time. Rushing to spill half researched findings would do no one any good."

"Did you really think we would let any of you outside into society?" The doctor asked. "As if nothing had changed?" He turned to Donnie who had come up to the platform and joined them. "You are a whole other issue."

"What does that mean?" Paul asked.

"We cannot allow you to take your son who can teleport all over the place away from this compound. He will remain here under observation and for obvious safety reasons." The liaison gave a little smile.

"The hell you say!" Chuck had to forcibly push Paul back.

"How about a compromise?" The liaison interjected.

"As opposed to keeping us prisoner? Still?" Paul replied vehemently.

"You know this neighborhood is under our control. The only ones living here are a few of the office workers and myself," the doctor said.

"How about we let you live within the factory neighborhood," the liaison began.

"While we continue to slave for you," Robyn added.

"And remain under our observation," the liaison finished.

"We would be neighbors," the doctor cooed.

"Then when will this be made public? I want in on it," Robyn demanded.

"Always the investigative journalist." The liaison stepped towards him. "We don't have enough information and just so you know, we are not the only facility."

"That's…"

"Have a little patience. I promise you, it will be well worth it."

Robyn tilted his head to one side and stared at the liaison who in turn gave a look of conviction. He contemplated all the points made and decided to see how it would all play out. Alex frowned, seeing his thoughts. It damn well better be worth it.

PRIZED COLLECTIONS

Professor Lancaster took in the interior of the monstrosity that would be one of the holding facilities for the half breed children as the lab technicians in charge gave him a tour. Everything was white, including the equipment and it hurt his eyes. It was much better than the old manufacturing warehouses his colleagues had previously acquired. Reconfiguring them was a pain in the ass and they still had to find a medical lab in the city for conducting research experiments.

It had already been twenty-five years since the alien ships crash landed and the oldest offspring were between eighteen and twenty-two. The data on them was fascinating yet frightening and for some their I.Q. was off the charts. His colleagues decided to call them Bi-Genetic children as a way keep simplify what they were.

A few of the newborns had died before the doctors figured out the timing when pulling the dark bloody membrane from the nostrils and mouth so they could breathe. The children also appeared to have a psychic bond with their parents and both could feel the other's pain.

Confirmation of this came during a routine quarantine of a mother and child when one of the technicians had slammed the small boy's head into a wall. The mother collapsed at the same moment, even though she was on the other side of the building. Death of either was more devastating. If the parents died, the child became an empty shell devoid of all emotion and if they somehow retained any emotion it was hatred. On the other hand, if the child died, then the parents became catatonic for a few weeks before recovering.

Some of the male children began to shift gender between the ages of ten and twelve, beginning menstrual cycles that occurred maybe two to three times year. Professor Lancaster approved a breeding project for when they reached the age of fifteen and he now stood in front of a bay window looking into a room filled with female teenagers laying sedated on hospital beds. He felt a tug of regret. Rapping on the window to first get the doctor on duty's attention he swiped his key card on the door's indicator and walked down the ramp into the bay.

"Good afternoon, Professor Lancaster," the female doctor greeted him as she approached.

"Afternoon, Dr. Strayer. What new information do we have this time?"

"Oh," she started, her eyes lighting up, "you are going to love this. There is just so much new data. I can't believe this was kept from us for so long."

They went to her desk and sat in front of the monitor. She typed in her code and pulled up the recent data from the combined last four years of research sent over from the old facility. An assortment of DNA strands was displayed.

"What exactly am I looking at, Doctor?"

"Okay, so we tried to impregnate as many as possible but there were some strange occurrences. Some of them got deathly ill, some miscarried almost immediately and others came through fine."

"When you say deathly ill..." Professor Lancaster began to ask.

"There were a few deaths, regrettably."

"Why?"

"Getting to that, Professor, but first let me tell you about the incubation period."

"Alright."

"Half!"

"Excuse me?"

Professor Lancaster sat back away from her.

"A normal human female takes nine months. These Bi-Genetics are exactly half the time. Four and a half months to the day! Exciting, huh?"

"Yes," he nodded and his mouth widened into a smile. "Tell me more."

"Well, this is the coup de grace." She tapped on her monitor at the DNA strands. "The reason some took and others did not is because their biology is DNA specific."

"Come again?"

"They can only get pregnant by someone with compatible DNA. The ones who died were the result of a DNA being toxic to their system."

Professor Lancaster's head was swimming with the information and what the possibilities were for his research. His regrets about approving the project faded.

"Fantastic," he whispered softly. He saw Dr. Strayer's impatience. "What else?"

"When we ran a simulation, we found that not only is it DNA specific but that there are only five compatible candidates on the planet for each individual. They look like a curve. The most compatible is on one end, there's a backup, then neutral in the middle. On the other end are the ones who are toxic."

"The implications. It's like they have their own population control built into their DNA. No unwanted or accidental pregnancies."

"Wait! There's more!" Dr. Strayer exclaimed.

"You're killing me. What else?"

"This."

She typed in a file name and the image displayed was an elongated membrane with what appeared to be small lights twinkling on and off along its sides. The image rotated at different angles giving them a 3D view.

"We call it a pressure point cylinder. It's what controls a lot of their biological functions, including shifting gender."

"How does it work, exactly for shifting?"

"You can either hit the pressure point directly, it's located just above the left hip before the bone, or electric current."

"Electric current?" Professor Lancaster did not like the sound of that.

"We had one of them get a little violent. Granted, he was under a lot stress. We decided to give him shock therapy. We monitor everything here so it was a surprise when his pressure point cylinder lit up with each jolt and he shifted involuntarily."

"Hmm." Professor Lancaster tapped his lower lip with a finger. "Those are the only two ways?" Dr. Strayer frowned. "Tell me."

"Bodily harm." She turned to him and sighed heavily. "I can tell you some of the workers here afraid of these children and have done things we should not tolerate. Three orderlies beat one of the younger boys, resulting in broken bones and fractured ribs. To protect itself, the body shifted, since their female form can withstand pain three times that of its male side. The orderlies took it as an invitation to…" Dr. Strayer stopped talking.

Professor Lancaster went pale.

"Where are these orderlies? Don't tell me they are still here!" This was not to be tolerated indeed.

"Where would we send them? They have classified

information not known to the public. How are we to contain them?"

He became aware that whatever she saw in his eyes frightened her.

"Leave that to me. Give my assistants the information." He stood up and headed for the exit. "Thank you, Dr. Strayer. I look forward to more great things from you."

Back in the hall with his entourage of lab assistants and renovators, he continued the walk through. He was impressed by its size considering where it was located. Even that was a secret the government didn't need to know. Stopping in what would serve as the cafeteria, he turned to one of the renovators.

"How will this facility be configured?"

"Dorm style. We can fit six to a room and have ten rooms per sector. That way the section monitors are not overwhelmed. We just need to know how to select who goes with who in each room."

"That has already been decided. Do we have a containment area?"

"Of course. It is reinforced new material derived from the alien ships. Stronger than titanium."

"Excellent. How long before the facility is complete?"

"Right now, we are ahead of schedule so, within the year." The renovator dropped his arm holding his notepad. "We need someone to run this monster."

"That too has already been decided. He should be here before completion to help facilitate the intake process."

"A fellow colleague of yours?"

"No," Professor Lancaster smiled, "A Bi-Genetic who happened to slip through the cracks attending medical school." He resumed walking and stopped a few yards later realizing his entourage had not followed. "Come, we have work to do."

PRISONER FOR SCIENCE

Five Years Before

The patient lay face down on the operating table heavily sedated while the surgeons tried to decide what to do with him first. His head had been shaved bald and a deep brown stripe two inches wide ran down the length of his spine from the tail bone up to the back of his skull. One of the surgeons produced a large needle and nodded. The others nodded in response and the patient was flipped over on his back. With slow precision, the needle was inserted under his chin and up into the brain to extract a watery illuminating white fluid.

A storm brewing outside gained momentum and the needle was removed just as a clap of thunder shook the room, making the lights flicker. Only a few drops of the fluid spilled as it was transferred into a vial for immediate storage. His colleagues frowned at his sloppiness but it was successful.

"All we want is for you to show us the girl. You could end this now." The head surgeon spoke to the patient when there would obviously be no response. Turning to his assistant he said, "Take him up."

She responded by gesturing the two orderlies with her hand to retrieve the gurney. They jumped into action gently lifting the patient and repositing him effortlessly. The other surgeons exited the operating chamber,

72

discarding gloves and face masks in the waste receptacle. They waited until the two orderlies pushed the gurney onto the elevator and its doors closed before heading to the conference room. Despite routine cleanliness the place was still dingy. The facility used to be an old warehouse with a printing press on the other side. Not ideal for medical research but they made do.

"Why doesn't he just tell us?" A young female intern asked, scratching her head.

"He probably doesn't want to begin a cycle that he can't stop. He doesn't want to become a guinea pig for the sake of science." One of the male surgeons voiced his guess.

"Well, he's already that," another male surgeon snorted.

"Once he changes, his whole world will shatter," the head surgeon chimed in.

"Change?" The female intern was puzzled.

"He's not human, you know that."

"Yes, but change into what?"

The head surgeon smiled. He had to thank Professor Lancaster for approving this project when it was over. He was having fun. Glancing over at the others, he replied.

"You will know soon enough."

In his cell, the patient sat rocking back and forth at the head of the bed, tears streaming down his face. The dark birth mark on his spine grew darker from increased blood flow. The words of the head surgeon kept running around over and over in his head.

"Show us the girl? Where's the girl? What girl? Who did they want? And, why should he know?"

He laid on his side and curled up in a ball. Exhaustion took over and he drifted off into sleep.

A knock on the door days later made him jolt awake

and as he pushed himself up, it opened. The head surgeon entered the room followed by a female nurse carrying a large needle. The sight of the needle was enough to put the patient in a state of panic. He started shaking his head wildly.

"No! No! No, no, no, no!"

"Time for your weekly dose."

The doctor and nurse held him down while the needle was pushed into his arm injecting a muscle relaxer. It took effect quickly and the patient's struggles weakened. Once the needle was out, the nurse left doctor and patient alone.

"Show me the girl" The doctor requested again.

"I don't…know…what," the patient's speech slurred, "…you want."

Smiling, the doctor climbed onto the bed and leaned over him.

"We want you."

"I don't…under…stand." The patient's eyes rolled up in their sockets.

The doctor pressed his body against him and the patient, not wanting to touch him, hesitated to push him away.

"Go ahead, touch me." The doctor whispered softly. "I won't hurt you. Try to push me off, if you can." He watched shaky hands push into his chest. "See? It's okay."

The drug was taking affect so the doctor maneuvered his hand to the sweet spot that triggered the patient's pressure point cylinder and slowly pressed deep into it. He heard a sharp intake of air escape the patient's lips before his body began to shift. The doctor laid a hand above the patient's heart and feeling the breasts form.

"You're so very warm." He removed the hospital gown in one motion and stared down at the patient. "See, you found the girl." The patient glanced at their now female body and tried once again to push the doctor off. He could see the despair surfacing in her glazed eyes while he took off his scrubs.

"Remember this time." The head surgeon grabbed her thighs and opened them wide. He entered her roughly, relishing in her puny cries of pain.

It was the same every time. He would bring out the female side of the patient, force himself on her then take her down for more testing. Electric shock instantly reverted the patient back into male stage never remembering anything that happened before. The doctor grinned. As long as he was got his fill in conjunction with valid data, he couldn't care less about code of ethics.

Back in his room after another series of tests which included more needles, the patient sat on the bed leaning against the headboard staring into nothingness. Drool trickled out the corner of his mouth and the doctor wiped it away.

"You worked so hard to come here for residency and here you are. Not what you had in mind was it? Well, you will be living here until our studies are complete. How does another two years of residency sound?"

Just as the doctor stepped out the door and into the hallway, the patient snapped out of his reverie and screamed.

"No! Let me go!"

He stopped to answer him. "I can't do that. I won't let you go. Not yet." Continuing, he waved a hand at the distraught patient.

The door shut and an electronic click sounded. The patient flopped forward on his hands and knees, sobbing.

After a year and six months of secretly forcing himself on his patient and training his body to shift on its own, the head surgeon decided it was time to show off the progress made. Three other doctors and four nurses sat watching the silent and unresponsive patient strapped down to a chair in front of them. He was roused up, clearly frightened of what they might do to him this time. The head surgeon leaned close to him with a smile on his face and made the usual request.

"Show us the girl"

The patient shuddered and his head shook left to right.

"No," he whispered.

Everyone sat up a little straighter and glanced around at each other, then the head surgeon. The patient continued to utter the word 'no'.

"This is a totally different response from before, doctor. I don't know if it's a good thing or a bad one. The questions about the girl seems to have taken a toll on him psychologically."

"I knew he would crack sooner or later," a nurse commented.

The head surgeon smiled again and knelt in front of his patient.

"What do you remember?"

"No," he whispered again.

"What do you remember?" He was so close they breathed the same air.

"You," the patient finally said. "I remember you."

"Really? What about me do you remember?"

"I remember you inside me, touching me."

The doctor stood up and backed away so not to obstruct his colleagues view.

"Show us the girl and it will all be over. I promise you." Their eyes locked.

With eyes squeezed shut, tears streaming down his face, the patient forced his body to shift. A painful three minutes of transformation commenced. With drugs, it had only taken a mere twenty seconds. As each body part rearranged itself, the patient screamed in agony. The head surgeon winced, feeling some sympathy for his charge. Shift completed, body drenched in sweat, the patient threw their head back.

"Colleagues," the head surgeon announced, "the girl." He stood arms out wide in exaltation, his witnesses sitting in stunned realization at the breakthrough after years of research. Seeing his patient crying and exhausted, he went to kneel back in front of her. "Congratulations, Doctor Bartley, you passed."

Puzzled, the patient tried to lift her head to see what he meant but her body seemed heavy. All her strength had been drained. The only thing keeping her in the chair were the restraints.

"Come with me."

The doctor undid the straps and lifted her up off the chair. He carried her back to the room that had served as a prison cell for nearly two and a half years so she could rest.

The head surgeon and Dr. Bartley donned white lab coats and sat in front of a computer monitor in the research wing. Slamming a huge binder filled with reports down in front of him, the head surgeon smiled.

"Read it. When you're done, there are three more and some lab work has to be done."

Dr. Bartley just stared at it. He was drained of everything; Pride, humanity, energy. What was supposed to be a great residency opportunity turned out to be a nightmare.

He didn't want any part of it.

"What happened before, especially between us, is

past. Never to be revisited again. This is now." With that, he left him alone in the lab.

Flipping open the binder he read the first report which included government medical files on a new evolution of humans. As he kept reading, everything became clear.

When he applied for the internship, he had to go through a thorough medical screening. He concluded that's how they knew he was one of the evolved humans. In order to get him as a test subject, the deal was sweetened with an advancement of his professional license. The facility made good on it. He would now be a professor but he wondered if the horrors he suffered by the hands of the head surgeon were worth it.

One small notation in the second binder regarding the dark brown birth mark on his spine caught his attention. 'No known reason for foreign attached membrane'. He smirked. The answer would be found by him alone and he vowed to never let them know once he did.

"Congratulations, Dr. Bartley!" the head surgeon exclaimed. "You have now graduated to the status of scientist. All you have to do is read over these documents and come to your party."

The cover of the document had Bi-Genetic Research in bold letters across it. Dr. Bartley looked up at him. "Is this an updated report?"

"Your five-year residency is up." He dodged the question. "So, what did you think?"

"That you're a sadistic bastard who should never be allowed to practice medicine."

"Hmm. You may be right, but that's a moot point, isn't it?" The head surgeon left the room.

"Colleagues! I give you Professor Bartley!"

Everyone in the room stood up clapping then

grabbed their drinks to raise in the air. Professor Bartley slowly picked his up and raised it as well, not feeling in a joyous mood. He was tired, angry and indifferent towards them all at once.

"Welcome to the new era of science!" One of the bastards yelled at him from the back of the room with a drunken smile on his face.

The head surgeon pulled him aside an hour into the festivities and gestured to one of the empty rooms. Apprehensive, Professor Bartley shook his head. Exasperated, the doctor grabbed his arm and shoved him in.

"Stop being childish."

"You shouldn't be surprised," Professor Bartley spat.

"Noted," the doctor sighed heavily. "There is a new government program with a cutting-edge facility ready to break ground. I think you would be perfect for it. You would be on the cusp of every major advancement in medical technology."

"Why me?"

"Because you're qualified to handle beings like yourself."

Professor Bartley resented the assumption that he was not human.

"So, this installation would be strictly for Bi-Genetics?"

"Of course. Just like this one used to be. You could send the younger ones here for us to examine."

The doctor's smile was sinister.

"No." Professor Bartley would never forget his three years of torment.

"Then, you'll take it?"

"Will I run it?"

"Exclusively. It will be yours to do as you wish."

"No one will interfere?"

It sounded too good to be true.

"No. As I said, it will be yours to run."

"When can I leave?"

"Are you in a hurry?" The doctor laughed.

Not laughing, Professor Bartley looked him square in the face and answered, "Yes."

Corporate Labs R&D

Yellow pinpoints from the street lights pierced through the dark tint of Sawyer's sunglasses as the bus rolled down the main thoroughfare. He sat in the window facing seats near the front behind the driver so he could check the road signs at each stop. Another barrage of light beams flashed into his retinas making him wince. His eyes had become sensitive to light in just the past few months forcing him to wear dark shades even at night.

Other passengers glanced at him with varied looks of distaste. It made him feel more self-conscious. He even caught the driver's reflection in the rear-view mirror look up at him questioningly. Sawyer ran his fingers through his thick mop of wavy, chocolate brown hair. His grey t-shirt and black jeans were loose fitting for comfort and his sneakers were dingy. Where he was heading did not give him the sense of needing to impress anyone.

He was going to see his mother. She had remarried over a year ago but he refused to attend the ceremony or meet the man. Why would she do this so late in life? Granted, she was alone since his father died when he was around ten. Sawyer thought being widowed for so long, she would have just accepted her fate. A familiar landmark came into view and he pulled the signal to stop as he stood. At five feet eleven he was of average height for a guy, practically unnoticeable.

The bus stopped at the corner and Sawyer waited at the top of the steps for the doors to open. When the driver did so, he gave the man a nod.

"Thank you."

The driver gave him a dirty look and didn't respond.

Sawyer stepped onto the sidewalk wet from rain and looked around. The bus sped off, splashing water upwards a few feet from him. The weather was warm for February so he hadn't bothered to bring a jacket. He adjusted his sunglasses. Night time in the city was never dark nor silent due to the businesses booming and lights everywhere. Not five blocks away sat a residential area, mostly brick apartment buildings five stories high. One of them was his destination.

Walking up the stairs of his mother's complex, he went over in his mind what he should say. He hesitated to push the buzzer next to her new last name but took a deep breath and did it. The noise grated on his ears. It was way too loud and surely someone had complained about it already. Of course, the landlord probably didn't care. A crackling voice followed.

"Yes?"

"It's me," Sawyer replied softly.

"Oh. Come on up."

He heard the buzz click of the door and pushed through into the lobby. Directly to his right were long steep stairs and an elevator. He contemplated taking the stairs to stall for time but decided the quicker the better so took the elevator. On the ride to the fourth floor, he removed his shades and hung them on the front of his shirt. The doors parted to reveal a dimly lit hallway with vintage decorative carpeting of dark red and gold. At the third door, he knocked twice. It flew open wide and his mother stood before him.

She was still a bit too plump for her full figured height, which was equal to his, and did her no favors. Her dirty blond hair was thick, frizzy and hung loose down to her waist. The button-down dress she wore strained against her bosom. Small gaps became visible where the buttons were on the verge of giving way. His mother gave him a forced smile. He returned one of his own. They hugged awkwardly before she motioned him in, shutting the door.

In a wheelchair to his left was her new husband. An older black man in a navy-blue suit, the front of his hairline peppered with gray. Ahead of them was the dining table set off from the kitchen already set for three. He could see the casserole dish brimming with homemade bacon sprinkled mac and cheese; his favorite. Off to the side on the counter, he spotted a prescription bottle and from the name, knew the medication was for diabetics. Sawyer glanced at the older man who greeted him with a thin smile.

He had seen it many times before in his profession. Diabetics were not too fond of letting go of the good stuff regardless of their condition. In this case, it made him feel a little better knowing someone else could appreciate his mother's cooking magic.

"Come on, sit down. The foods getting cold."

His mother made her way around her husband's wheelchair and pushed him to the spot next to the head of the table.

Once they were all together, she held out her hands for them to hold. At first, he was confused, his mother never having done that before. Then he realized why. He clasped hers and slowly took her husband's. Joined by physical contact, his mother began prayer.

"Thank you, lord, for bringing us together for this great meal. May it nourish our hearts and souls. Amen."

"Amen," her husband said.

"Amen," Sawyer whispered.

His mother passed each dish to let everyone take their fill. While they ate, the small talk commenced.

"How are things going at the lab, sweetie?"

Sawyer waited until he was done chewing before answering.

"The work load is ramping up. My team is keeping up."

"Aren't they going to promote you any time soon?"

"You mean become a project manager?"

"Yes! I think you would be great at it."

"It's a lot of work, mom."

"Oh, pooh!" She waved her hand across her face. "You can handle it."

Her husband simply nodded then took another forkful of mustard greens.

"Maybe in another year or so."

Sawyer squinted at his plate to clear his vision. Some days he got headaches with blurred view but on the flip side he would have better than 20/20.

"Is there something wrong with your eyes?" His mother asked.

"Hmm. Just a bit."

"I noticed you have your sunglasses and it's dark outside."

He saw the look of worry on her face and smiled.

"It only bothers me sometimes." She frowned. "Really, I'm okay."

The meal continued with minimal discussion and he thanked the heavens for that.

After helping his mother clean up the dishes, Sawyer shook hands with his new stepfather and kissed his mother on the cheek.

"Can't you stay a bit longer?"

"I have to get to the lab early, so no."

"Will you come visit again?"

He was thrown by the sorrowful tone in her voice. She was hurt by him not accepting her decision, he could see that now.

"Yeah, mom. Of course."

"Don't be a stranger," his stepfather called out.

"I won't."

Giving her another kiss, he left the modest apartment.

Back in the hallway, the dim lights were like tiny suns burning his retinas. He took his shades off his shirt and put them on. They gave him some reprieve, enough to get him through the ride home. Taking the bus made the trip twice as long but he didn't want to risk driving with his sight impaired. People on the bus stared at him yet again as he showed the driver his pass and sat down. He dozed off for the long trip.

Sawyer got off the bus and walked three blocks to his home. The street lamps were on to guide him safely towards his building. He climbed the stairs to the second floor and dug his key out of his pocket. Once inside, he found it pitch dark but decided not to turn on the lights. Tossing his sunglasses on the kitchen counter, he started down the corridor to the bedroom.

It was even darker and that suited his aching eyes. He stripped down to his underwear and crawled under the covers. Not quite comfortable, he moved further towards the middle of the bed until there was soft resistance. His boyfriend stirred.

"Sorry," Sawyer whispered.

"S'okay. How'd it go?"

"Fine."

"Sawyer," his boyfriend sighed impatiently.

"Findley."

He snuggled closer. Findley reached over and stroked his thigh.

"Go to sleep, baby."

Sawyer closed his eyes and drifted off.

The alarm shrieked at six a.m. jolting both men awake. Findley slowly sat up, only to be stopped halfway by the weight of Sawyer partially draped across him. That was as far as he had gotten as well. Now able to somewhat function, he slammed a hand down on the top of the alarm clock, cutting the ruckus off. He raised Sawyer's head off his abdomen and kissed him good morning before getting a good look at him. Exhaustion etched his beautiful face and his eyes were blood shot.

"Come on, babe. We gotta' take a shower and get ready for work." Sawyer responded with a strangled grunt. "I know you're tired." He caressed his back. "I know."

When Sawyer began to whimper, followed by soft wailing, it scared Findley. That was not normal behavior for his lover. The hours in the lab were long and grueling but they both handled it so far. He did consider the stress factor of Sawyer going to see his mother.

"I'm so tired," Sawyer cried.

"Shh."

Findley swung his legs off the bed and stood, gathering Sawyer in his arms. He carried him into the bathroom and laid him in the tub. The underwear came off with one tug followed by Findley baring all. He turned on the shower and stepped in just as Sawyer reared up, gasping in surprise.

"Isn't that better?"

Sawyer leaned forward and let the hot water drench him.

"Yeah."

Findley held the exfoliating puff in one hand while he squeezed body wash onto it. Time for a scrub down.

Findley got in the driver's seat of their compact car and looked over at Sawyer. He was slumped in the passenger side with his eyes closed. Furrows on his brow let

Findley know the headache hadn't gone away. There were also the shades. Something was definitely wrong and he needed to keep a better eye on his love. The clock on the dash clicked over and he started the car. They were going to be late if he dallied any longer. He could stare at Sawyer's beautiful face for hours if time permitted.

Twenty minutes later, he eased the car into the middle lane of the security checkpoint for their building. The large skyscraper in the city's industrial sector housed government scientists researching different technologies and medical breakthroughs due to alien indoctrination. Labs took up floors four through twelve. He had no idea what occupied the rest of the twenty-story structure. At the guard shack, he handed the man Sawyer's keycard then his own. The familiar beep sounded for each one and the bar lifted right as the guard handed them back. He found a spot on the garage's sixth floor which meant they could take the sky walk right into their lab's main area. With a gentle nudge, he got Sawyer to sit up.

"Doing okay?"

"Yeah." He took off his sunglasses and winced. "Just give me a second."

Findley could see his eyes dilate then restrict and the pained look disappeared.

"Are you sure?"

"Perfect vison."

Sawyer opened the car door and got out.

That's the problem. Findley said to himself.

Sawyer never had perfect vision until six months ago.

Once inside, they split up and headed to their departments. Findley swiped his card on the reader to open the glass double doors for the lab he worked in. Five other technicians did research along with him and they were already at their stations.

He checked his watch to confirm that he wasn't late. "What brings you all here so early?"

"Did you forget? Lancaster Junior is coming to check on our progress this afternoon. I'd rather have this one," his female colleague pointed at the beakers in front of her, "completed before he gets here."

"Oh. That," Findley replied deadpan.

Dr. Lancaster was on the fast track to be a professor like his older brother. He had been put in charge of the research building to work on the top-secret Bi-Genetic phenomenon that the public had no knowledge of. Findley despised him. For obvious reasons and one personal. Having his work scrutinized by a pariah like Lancaster irked him. Most people hadn't notice, but he saw the madness in him. A hunger for more research on the hybrid humans that did not translate into being good for mankind. It was a selfish need.

"Well," a male colleague sighed. "Let's get this done and show the man some data."

Findley snorted but went to his station to finish the blood analysis he had started yesterday.

At lunchtime, Findley headed down to the cafeteria on the first floor to meet Sawyer. He was sitting at one of the curved counters midway from the doors. The corners of his eyes were wrinkled and he seemed to squint at the writing on his cup. Findley became worried again.

"Hey there," he said while sliding into the seat next to him. He swiveled around so that they were face to face and Sawyer peered up at him. His eyes were glassy. "How you feeling?"

"Okay," Sawyer replied softly.

Pulling his hair back with both hands, Findley clasped them together and gave Sawyer a quizzical look.

"Really?"

Loud voices broke their focus as a flood of people came through from off the elevators. They paid it no mind after realizing what it was, which set them up to be startled.

"Good afternoon, kids!"

Dr. Lancaster slapped his hands on their shoulders and leaned in a little.

"Doctor," Sawyer said cheerily.

"Aww, you know you don't have to call me that." He stood up straight and removed his hands. With one, he cupped the side of Sawyer's face and stared deep into his eyes. "You feeling okay, sweetness?"

Findley grabbed Dr. Lancaster's wrist and pulled it away.

"Don't." The two men made eye contact.

"I'm fine," Sawyer said. "Just tired these days."

"They aren't working you too hard, are they?" Dr. Lancaster asked as he averted from Findley's stare.

"That would be you, if so. These are your projects we're working on."

"Stop," Sawyer pleaded. He held his forehead and leaned against the counter.

Feeling childish, Findley reached over and caressed his head.

"I'll get you some water."

As he stood up, Dr. Lancaster stepped back.

"I'll check in on you later, okay?" He said to Sawyer.

Both men walked off towards the cashier station, maneuvering through the now crowded cafeteria.

"Just because you had a relationship with him first doesn't mean you can touch him like that," Findley said.

"Then you should take care of him better," Dr. Lancaster retorted. Findley balled his hands into fists, fighting the urge to sock him. "I'll take a mineral water," he addressed the hostess behind the register. To Findley he said, "See you after lunch for your team's evaluation."

When Lancaster was back on the elevator and the doors closed, Findley unclenched his hands and took a deep breath. He ordered food for Sawyer and himself with two waters then went to sit with Sawyer who was not doing so well.

Sawyer came out of the bathroom and ran into Dr. Lancaster. It was past two in the afternoon and everyone was getting antsy as the day neared closing. He stepped back to make room between them.

"Hey kiddo," Lancaster greeted him with a smile. "You mind walking with me?"

"No, not at all." Sawyer let him spin him around by the shoulders.

They made their way down the hall and ended up in Dr. Lancaster's office.

"Now," he breathed out. "Tell me the truth."

At that, Sawyer was taken off guard. But he knew what he meant.

"I just...I'm mentally exhausted is all."

"But why?"

Lancaster's gaze seemed to penetrate him.

"I went to see my mother and her new husband the other day."

Dr. Lancaster's eyes narrowed.

"Why? Why would you do that? That's too much stress on you right now."

"I didn't want to avoid it anymore," Sawyer snapped.

"And, so?" he asked, sighing heavily.

"It was fine." Sawyer leaned on the wall.

Dr. Lancaster moved to stand in front of him and cupped his hands around Sawyer's face.

"I do miss you."

"But that's not enough. Your research is more important, and I know that."

"It is. I can only focus on that right now. But, that doesn't mean I don't worry about you."

Before Sawyer could stop him, he gently kissed him on the lips. They lingered there for a while before he disengaged.

"He really should take better care of you."

Sawyer backed out of his office and headed back to his lab. His vision blurred but he didn't stop, fearing Lancaster might notice.

They're surfacing.

Dr. Lancaster sat on the edge of his desk and mentally ran an analysis of what he saw in Sawyer's eyes. Multiple tests had shown that whatever latent power he had was dormant. For it to begin revealing itself at such a late age meant something triggered it. Instantaneously. Sharp glimmers of shine like mini suns pulsed, dancing around Sawyer's irises. He had no clue as to what kind of power his former lover would have but it didn't matter. The thought made his scientist juices flow, giving him an erection that his pants barely contained.

"Ah, Sawyer. I want to desecrate you in every way."

The taste of his lips still present lingered so he licked his own, letting his head fall back.

Home after maneuvering through massive traffic, Findley and Sawyer dropped down onto the couch and sat still, heads touching. The sun was just starting to lower itself for the evening. Neither one wanted to move but knew someone would have to make dinner.

"What do have a taste for?" Findley asked.

He moved his hair over to the other side so it would block Sawyer's face.

"Hmm. Not sure. Something light."

"That's been a given for a while now. What happened to having a good juicy steak?"

He watched Sawyer's face contort and throat bob. An illness colored his cheeks and Findley sat back.

"What's wrong?"

Sawyer shook his head then without warning spewed vomit all over the coffee table, rug and himself. Findley immediately held his head steady, making sure his hair was out of the way.

"Ahh, baby, what is going on?"

Sawyer let out a gasp and began crying. The tears blended into the splatter vomit.

"I can't see! It hurts!"

Findley brought him close then he noticed movement on the rug. He looked down and saw white hot beams of light burn into the aftermath, making it sizzle. The smell nearly made him gag but he didn't dare move. When the light died out, he realized where it had come from.

Shit!

He knew. And if that bastard Lancaster was any real scientist, he would have noticed too. Sawyer was in danger. But first, he had to know why now.

❧

Getting a medical checkup appointment on short notice and in secret was no easy task, so he tapped an acquaintance unaffiliated with the research company. They were quite adamant in demanding all personnel use the medical facilities on campus. Findley also concluded it was mostly for collecting data. Sawyer had gotten worse over the course of a week, bad enough that he shifted during another episode. By the second week, Sawyer could no longer shift back.

They got out of the car in front of a hospital thirty miles from home. Findley figured it was a good enough distance and wouldn't arise suspicion. If he had it his way, they would have gone to the next state over. This hospital was also keeping the secret of hybrids but did intake based on credentials.

"Come on, sweetheart. We gotta' go in."

Sawyer was already pretty but in female form, a real beauty in his opinion. Perfectly round breasts, soft skin and an ass that was not quite toned but well endowed. She used the car as balance to come around to the other side next to him. Findley wrapped his arm around her and they made their way inside.

He went to elevators and pushed the button for the tenth floor. The sensor blinked repeatedly, not letting the door close until Findley reluctantly pulled out his key card. The sensor picked up its signal and the doors shut. On the tenth floor, a nurse greeted them and took Sawyer away. His friend gave him a nod before following them. Findley sat down in the waiting room and slumped down in a sofa.

Two hours later, his friend woke him up and escorted him to a private room. Sawyer was on the hospital bed fast asleep. The pain lines that were etched on her face were gone and she looked like some angelic creature he wanted to save.

"We had to sedate her," the doctor said.

"What?" Findley shook off his fantasies. "Why?"

"She was in a lot of pain. Those eyes are…something."

"Why has this happened? She was fine until six months ago."

"You know how a Bi-Genetic can delay gestation for months on end?"

"Huh? What does that have to do with…"

"When was the last time you had sex with your mate in female stage?"

"Like," Findley was trying to think.

"She's been pregnant for the past six months but since she hasn't shifted, the fetus has been in stasis." Findley's eyes went wide. Fear, anxiety and astonishment coursed through him. "Her pregnancy is going to advance rapidly. That is what awakened her dormant abilities." The doctor eyed him curiously. "Which brings me to my next question."

"Don't," Findley ordered. He snapped back to his senses and gave his friend a warning stare.

"Figured as much." The doctor got close to him. "You can't hide her or any of this for much longer. He's a bit possessive, you know."

"More than you think."

"Good luck."

The doctor left them in the room and Findley slapped both hands against his face, keeping them there. He grabbed the edges of his hair and let out a strangled cry.

It was inevitable, but Findley still tried to keep Dr. Lancaster from seeing Sawyer. He did it for about a month while the doctor was at a training seminar out of state. Sawyer was showing, her time equivalent to the start of second trimester from holding it back so long. Rapid was an understatement. She had another month and half to go. There was no way Dr. Lancaster didn't know. He came out of his lab to see the doctor head towards Sawyer's department. Of course, his first day back would mean a visit to see his former lover. Findley chewed his tongue so he wouldn't call out to stop him. There was no turning back now.

⤺

Sawyer nearly dropped the test tube in her hand when Dr. Lancaster came strolling into her lab, greeting her colleagues as he made a beeline for her. He halted in front of her and raised his arms, opening them wide. He wanted a hug. She carefully pushed herself off the stool and went to him.

His arms wrapped around her and squeezed, then stopped. He gently let go and moved her a few inches away from him. His stare trailed down to her swelled belly.

"Well, that's a surprise."

"It was the reason I wasn't feeling well," Sawyer laughed uncertain. "We're really shocked."

"Is that right?" He lifted her chin up so they could see each other clearly. "You're even more beautiful pregnant."

"Stop it," she blushed.

"I just wish it were mine."

The look in his eyes made her flinch. He used both hands to caress her hair and then arranged it neatly across her shoulders. A sudden pain hit behind her eyes and she winced, stepping farther away from him.

"What's wrong, sweetie? Here, sit back down."

Sawyer let him help her onto the stool and she kept her eyes closed until the pain subsided. When she opened them back, Dr. Lancaster smiled before planting a kiss on her forehead.

"Congratulations."

"Thanks."

"I," Dr. Lancaster began as he stood up, "have to go finish some paperwork in my office. You take care. I don't want you getting hurt in the lab."

"Don't worry, I'm being careful."

"Good. Talk to you soon."

Once he was gone, Sawyer shivered. That look was

frightening. She couldn't figure out why but she sensed danger. Which was crazy because he would never harm her.

Or would he?

In his office, Dr. Lancaster eased into his chair and leaned back in deep thought. Seeing Sawyer so far along made him angry and giddy simultaneously. If he had kept her for himself, putting the research on a back burner for a while, he was sure to have impregnated her sooner. Her powers showing up made more sense. That was the part that angered him. He found knowing Findley was indeed her true mate unacceptable. They had only been together two years whereas he had courted and mated with Sawyer since her college days.

Well, that's water under the bridge now.

The next step was to find a way to isolate her and keep the child in the research wing. Of course, the upside would be Sawyer at his constant disposal. A smile crept on his face. This was a break in his workings and the treasure trove of information he could get out of them would be endless for years to come. Findley needed to disappear.

The moment he saw the horror-stricken expression on Sawyer when he went to ask about her encounter with Dr. Lancaster, he sent her home. After the taxi pulled off, he went to the cafeteria and got a cup of coffee. He took a sip and realized he forgot the sugar. There was a container of it farther down the counter. Without looking, he held out his hand and the sugar slid right into it.

He was about to pour some in his cup when it dawned on him what just happened. Trying not to draw any more attention if there was any, he quickly scanned the room. Not many people were there and they seemed engrossed in their own conversations. Sighing with relief, he sweetened his coffee.

Someone did see. At the elevators, Dr. Lancaster stood rooted to the floor in front of the doors as he watched. By the way Findley did it nonchalantly, he concluded that the man knew of his own ability for quite some time. Everything clicked into place. A mate with powers already manifested would obviously jumpstart another. This also meant he couldn't get rid of Findley yet. Shaking off his awe, he advanced into the cafeteria.

"I see congratulations are in order," he said in Findley's ear.

Startled, Findley reared away from him. His gaze landing on him and a frown formed.

"Don't sneak up behind me."

"My apologies." Dr. Lancaster sat in the seat next to him. "I heard she went home early. Is everything alright?"

"She gets tired."

"I warned you to take better care of her."

Findley spun around to face him.

"I so take care of her. More than you ever could."

"Perhaps. But if you can't even manage that, I'll take her back."

"No, you won't! You research takes priority."

"That may be so, but I will sacrifice it if I have to."

Findley's face drained of color then flushed with anger. Dr. Lancaster got up and went to the register counter. He didn't mean to say that but he was resolved to do it. Findley chugged the rest of his coffee and left. The look on his face was priceless; fear.

⌒

The towel was too far to reach and he wasn't going to let go of Sawyer who lay half-conscious in his arms so Findley brought it to him telekinetically. He dried her off. She had fallen in the shower and luckily, he was behind her. Their unborn child was taking more than he should and he chided him often for it.

"See what you've done to your mother? Have a little restraint, will ya' kid?"

Sawyer opened her eyes and smiled up at him.

"Don't be mean," she whispered.

"Hey, we gotta' be firm on this or he'll keep doing." She laughed and he kissed her.

That night, she went into labor. Scared, Findley paced the floor trying to decide who to call. He finally contacted his friend's hospital and waited for the ambulance. The whole time, Sawyer screamed in pain, her eyes flickering white hot. When it arrived, they hurried her onto the stretcher and sped off. Findley sat next to her, letting her squeeze his hand.

The ambulance swerved on the road from something hitting it hard on its side. While the driver tried to correct it, another hit occurred and the vehicle tilted all the over. One of the paramedics help him keep Sawyer steady while the other braced for any impact. It skidded to a stop and the back doors flew open.

Four men in all black with ski masks stood holding assault rifles. Findley jumped up to raise a hand to push them away but wasn't fast enough. Two bullets hit him, slamming him against the back of the bus. The paramedics raised their hands in surrender and we shot anyway. Then two of the men came in and hauled a screaming Sawyer out into the night. From behind him he heard shouting and then a hard thud. He knew the driver had been taken out as well.

The sound of double doors being closed and Sawyer's screams cut off meant another ambulance had arrived. Findley focused as best he could ahead of him and saw the blurred logo of the research company.

You motherfuckers!

One of the paramedics was still breathing and so was he.

"Hold her down!" Dr. Lancaster ordered. One of the men was about to elbow her in the head. "You harm her, I'll kill you."

The man halted his movements and resumed applying pressure.

Sawyer's eyes burned with heat and hatred as she stared fixated on him. He didn't blame her. She should be angry. What woman wouldn't be in this situation. There was no remorse for what he had done. He did however hate the fact that his orders were not carried out specifically. When they came back without Findley and was told they'd shot him, not once, but twice, he was livid. How was he going to recreate another child without master DNA?

"Stop fighting. I don't want you to hurt yourself or your child."

"How could you? I will never forgive you!"

"I know." He stroked her head and she tried to get away from him. "I only want to keep you both safe." He smiled down at her. "With me. Always."

Hers eyes nearly bulged out of sockets then she screamed again. This time it frightened him. White light shot out from every orifice of her body as it arched up from the stretcher. The EKG went wild and he panicked.

"It's coming!" The nurse yelled. "We can't stop it. She's having her baby now!"

I'm going to lose her!

⌒

Barely patched up and feeling a bit woozy, Findley made his way up the stairs to the buzzer on the side of the brick building. The stolen car he kept running on the street since there was no key. He found the name of Sawyer's mother and hit the button.

"Yes?"

"It's Findley. Sawyer's boyfriend."

"Oh!"

The door buzzed and he put more effort into pushing it open despite the pain. He took the elevator up and knocked on the door when he got there. Sawyer's mother opened it and he stepped in. She looked at him for a long time, waiting. He leaned against the wall.

"Sawyer is in trouble."

"What do you mean?" She snapped at him.

Her hostility made him blink.

"We...Sawyer was pregnant." She clasped a hand over her mouth. "But you knew, he's different, right?" Tears streamed down her face and she nodded. "She went into labor. They took her." This time she became angry.

"Took her? Who took her?"

"Scientists. I tried..." Findley struggled to not cry himself. "I couldn't stop them, so I had to let them go."

Sawyer's mother advanced on him and began attacking him with both fists. Her husband came around the corner in his wheelchair and tried to calm her.

"Hey, now, sweetheart. Hold on."

"You let them take my child? You just stood there and watched?"

"Babe, please," her husband hollered.

Her yelling and fists blows were too much for him. Not able to really defend himself he slumped down to the floor and waited for her to stop.

"You let them just take her? My child, you," she

choked on the words then backed off him. Her hand went back to her mouth and she stifled her cries.

"I'll get her back," he whispered.

"What did you say?"

"I promise." Findley slowly slid up from the floor, using the wall for support. "I'll get her back. And our son."

He left her standing in the middle of her apartment and headed back down. There wasn't much time. Somewhere inside of him he could feel Sawyer slipping away along with new life psychically connecting to him emerge into the world.

Sawyer's mother rocked back and forth on her heels, hand still covering her mouth, until her view zeroed in on the wall where Findley had been. On the floor and halfway up the wall was a wide streaked of dark brownish red. Her hand fell away and she turned to her husband. He shook his head. Desperate, she ran down the stairs and got the street in time to see a car speed off. From the back of the driver's head she could tell it was him. At a loss, she went to her knees on the sidewalk and hugged herself.

Findley reached the rendezvous point outside the research building's dock adjacent to the medical wing. His doctor friend was already there waiting along with four others. There was some suspicion on what may happen if Dr. Lancaster got wind Sawyer was in labor but none of them ever expected this.

"How are you holding up?" His friend asked.

"Not too bad."

"You reopened your wounds. I can tell."

"You can fix me after."

"Fine. Let's get in, get out and find a safe place."

The group approached the inner yard.

Armed guards came flooding out.

"Not a step further. This is private property and we will use excessive force if nec…"

Findley made a motion with both hands and the dock doors seemed to warp outward then blasted open, leaving a gaping hole where they used to be. The guards were thrown in different directions and none of them landed nicely.

"Let's go," Findley said.

His friend's mouth turned up as he nodded in approval. "Nice."

Alarms went off. They were not deterred. Findley found out that the other four his friend brought also had powers so getting to the lower level of the building was easier than planned. Reaching the maternity ward, they were assaulted with pure white light that heated the whole corridor. Not wasting any more time, he burst through the glass doors and saw Sawyer lit up. From below, he could see his son's body half out but no nurse helping him. He saw why a second later as one of them tried to crawl away. Half the woman's body was burnt to a crisp and the others in the room were just as bad. Flames were all around near the equipment.

He went to Sawyer and somehow managed to get their son the rest of the way out. With two fingers, he inserted them in his nose and his pinky and thumb in his mouth to hooked onto the bloody tissue blocking the airways then yanked. It came out followed by the soft gasp of his newborn son take a breath for the first time. He wrapped him in the sheet, laid him on her chest then clasped her hand. She had stopped screaming and now looked down at their son. A smile formed on her face. She squeezed his hand back and pulled Findley close to her.

"I'm sorry," she whispered.

The light started to fade and an invisible knife pierced Findley's mind. It intensified the more the light dispersed and he pressed his head on her fingers. Before the light was completely gone, he kissed her with every bit of love he had for her. The pain in his head ceased as if cut off like a switch.

"No!" Dr. Lancaster came into the room from a side door. His singed clothes were the extent of damage he'd taken. "You can't have her!"

Findley picked up his son, still glowing from his birth and backed up.

"You monster, I'll kill you for this."

"That specimen you have in your hands belongs to my research."

More armed guards came flooding in and surrounded Findley and his group.

"My son," Findley said with gritted teeth, "is not your specimen."

"Fucking kill them and get me back what's mine!" Dr. Lancaster ordered.

Bullets came flying at them and Findley used his powers to push most of them away. The onslaught wouldn't let up and he still needed to protect his son. Something caught his eye above and a sphere of white light hovered. Without warning, it split in two, hitting him and his son. It knocked him back a good twenty feet away to his knees. Before the next barrage of bullets came he used his power and the flames in the room to create a backdraft.

Dr. Lancaster grabbed the end of the stretcher with Sawyer's body and went back out the side door. Findley cursed but didn't stop him. With Sawyer's power combined with his, he let loose and engulfed the entire room in an inferno. He could hear the screams of the guards as he ran out. His group had somehow survived the firing squad and were ahead of him. They made it outside to a safe distance right as the entire wing of the building went up in a mushroom cloud.

Findley held tight to his son who began to cry. He could feel his consciousness slipping away and his arms got weak. A van screeched to a halt in front of them and his friend became frantic.

"Hurry up! We can't lose him."

"Please, you have to take him," Findley cried softly.

A man came towards them and knelt.

"What's his name?"

Findley had a moment of clarity and grinned.

"Janti. His name is Janti."

"I'll take Janti, then."

He handed his son over to the man and his body gave in to the numbness, sliding sideways to ground. Sawyer's smiling face in her last moment of life flashed before him.

"I'm so sorry, Baby."

A dark blanket closed around him and he drifted into nothingness.

In her small apartment, Sawyer's mother clutched her chest and cried out in pain. She fell forward onto the kitchen floor and tried to catch her breath. An intense heat flared in her heart like it was being scorched away. Her mind had what she could only describe as a meat grinder having its way inside. The pain radiated through her whole being. Then it all stopped in an instant, leaving her hollow and numb.

"He's gone. My precious baby boy is gone."

Her husband wheeled over to her and leaned her head into his lap. Her eyes were wide open as she went into a catatonic state.

CHAPTER THREE

15 YEAR ITCH

A large group consisting of four news media crews, ten medical professionals, and six high level military personnel were led blindfolded down the long white corridor of Facility Three. Their sight had been handicapped in the transport vehicles as a prerequisite for the chance of a lifetime. Protests had arisen but were quickly quelled by the threat to cancel the trip for one of the rumored compounds housing evolved human species whose birth rate exploded in under two decades. Among the four journalists, was a now seasoned Robyn Laughlin.

The world had turned into a series of travesties as parents, either scared or disgusted at having a possible Biode, panicked and took advantage of the former top-secret program to remove the child from society. While some even went so far as to murder the infants outright, many waited to see if they were shifters before committing the deed. Those who could do neither, just dumped them in trash bins and dumpsters.

Media frenzy hit an all-time high as governments around the globe confirmed the origin of the newly evolved humans. For twelve years it was the top story and now the public would get a glimpse into the government machine to see what became of those abandoned children. Robyn was still feeling a bit raw about how long it took for the facilities to share information with each other for the greater good. He figured out pretty quick how it all worked but it left a bad taste. Even with all this, he still thought releasing the information sooner would have saved so many lives.

From his overhead view of the facility, Dr. Bartley watched over the procession with a feeling of sickness. He hated having them there to gawk and point at the children like animals in a zoo but had to comply to avoid an incident. Robyn caught his eye and he pursed his lips. The man had been released to start back reporting four years ago and he was like a dog with a bone. In all this time, he looked to have aged maybe five years. Robyn's editorials hit the mark every time because of his inside knowledge and the fact that he was fine tuned to telepathy. A nice side effect added to his talent. Resolved to the current event at hand, Dr. Bartley sat back and continued to watch his unwanted visitors.

Complete silence filled the space as everyone was forced to halt. One by one, the blindfolds were removed and the cameramen given their equipment back. In front of them was a solid white wall. Thin lines appeared, forming a long vertical rectangle and an opening was revealed. Standing in the entry way was a tall man with dark shoulder length hair wearing a white lab coat and wire rimmed glasses. His lips were pursed tight and his eyes shone with disdain for the group readying themselves for a freak show.

"This way." He stepped to one side allowing them to pass. As the last person went through the wall it became solid once again, shutting them off from where they entered. "Your feeds will have a slight delay due to the high security network here." With a sweep of his hand in the air towards the direction in front of them. "At your leisure."

The circus commenced as crews connected their gear and everyone began talking over each other until it reached a decibel level even too high for them. Another deathly silence came down hard. They had clearly forgotten where they were. Changing strategy, they spread out and broke into their respective groups, speaking just above whispers.

Another opening formed on the wall ahead of them revealing a staircase. One of the news anchors took the initiative and signaled his cameraman to roll.

"We are here at one of the research centers exclusively for the newly discovered advanced humans referred to as Bi-Genetics. A known fact kept secret for decades maybe even more. We are going to talk with the staff and if we're lucky a few of the patients here."

A fellow anchor tapped him on the shoulder when the feed paused.

"Not patients. I think they prefer the term residents."

"They're here against their will. That makes them prisoners in my book," another news anchor added.

A female reporter shivered. The stark white from the walls to the floors, even the equipment she caught a glimpse of below the stairs seemed to make her nervous. Engrossed in the scenery, she did not see the older man with dirty blonde bed head hair and a white lab coat ascend the stairs to greet the group.

"Good afternoon, ladies." He nodded at the visibly startled female reporter. "And gentlemen. My name is Professor Graham. I run the second stage program here but I will be escorting you to all the levels up to stage four." He turned back to the stairs. "If you'll follow me, please, all of you."

At the bottom of the stairs, the corridor was solid on one side with an endless array of bay windows on the other. Inside the windows were row after row of visibly distressed infants and small children in hospital chambers.

"This level, level one, is our intake where we process all the children. Sad cases, as we call them. People have their babies tested to find out if they may or may not have a Bi-Genetic trait before tossing them to us. They don't realize or understand that these babies are born fully aware of their parentage and rejection is physically painful.

"Wait," one of the medical doctors stopped him. "You mean if I give up a Bi-Genetic baby it knows who I am? So, they can potentially grow up to hate me?"

"Not hate," Professor Graham corrected him. "Just disappointed and sad." He moved on. "Once they are here, we do a series of tests. Blood, brain fluid, DNA, the works."

As everyone looked down into one of the bays, a cameraman zoomed in on a baby crying as a needle was pushed under its chin. Extracted fluid flowed into the syringe.

"Oh my God!" The female reporter screamed. "What are they doing?"

"As I said, brain fluid samples. It's one of the first steps for analysis."

"Horrible."

The cameraman shuddered and pulled away from the glass.

The group saw even more disturbing scenes as they moved through the level until they came to a lift big enough to accommodate them. A sensor recognized the last person to enter then sealed the doors shut before shooting upward. Getting off, they were greeted by yet another man in a white lab coat.

Smiling wide, the man introduced himself.

"Hi there! I'm Dr. Vasence. I help run stage two. Please, follow me." He saw the looks of dread on the group's faces and smirked. "On your left is the testing area. A lot of five-year olds show signs of high level intelligence so we gauge their I.Q."

Twenty or so children sat in a row strapped down in front of a monitor. They were being bombarded with a series of visual information. Their eyes were wide open as if in a trance. A few of the military men shook their heads in disbelief.

"Next up is my terrain."

He led them up four flights of stairs and the change in scenery was immediate. No stark white walls or equipment on this level. Peach colored interior with brown accent lit by yellow lights made the entire corridor look orange. In one of the bays sat a little boy of maybe seven hooked up to a formidable looking machine. His eyes were covered with some sort of helmet apparatus and tubes ran from various parts of his body.

"A select few show signs of what we call talent. It could be something banal like telepathy or something much more interesting. We try to do early detection and teach them how to control it."

"Isn't this a bit barbaric for a child?" A doctor in the group spoke up, horrified.

Dr. Vasence laughed and shook his head. "Not at all. It's a great way for them to burn calories. You see, Bi-Genetics using talent need at least ten thousand calories a day. Their system burns them quickly and if we were to try and do it the old-fashioned way, it would require excessive exercising. No, exercising the mind works best."

From his vidscreen, Dr. Bartley saw Robyn look up to stare directly into the hidden camera. That unnerved him. He really didn't want him in his facility casting judgement, let alone knowing where things were that no one else did.

Is this really how you run the place?

Robyn asked him telepathically.

Better than the others! You should know that."

Dr. Bartley snapped back.

Still doesn't make it right.

Professor Graham turned around to face the group so Robyn disengaged his stare and paid attention.

"Anyone hungry?" Professor Graham piped up.

"It's lunchtime."

The group was escorted down to below the first level and ended up in front of giant double doors. They were back in the stark white environment much to the groups' chagrin. As the doors swung open an onslaught of children's voices and the smell of food cooking greeted them.

"This is the cafeteria for ages eight to seventeen. As you can see, they are quite happy here." Dr. Vasence announced joyously.

"How come there are so many boys?" A colonel inquired.

"Most Bi-Genetics are born male. Some have the ability to change gender, hence the name." Professor Graham explained.

"Ahh," a few in the group said in unison.

"As you can also see, we make sure the older ones with talents are put to use. The kitchen and the serving line are run by the kids on duty. Think of it as fully automated and hands free. One of our more talented ones is Tommy."

At sixteen years old Tommy was tall with dark brown wavy hair past his shoulders that constantly flopped in his face no matter how many times he used his fingers to push it back. His eyes were the color of bronze and he deemed himself angelic, but with a sinister twist. Hearing his name, he turned to see the entourage of visitors and let out a loud sigh. Leaning against the galley wall he flipped burgers, baked cakes and served food all at the same time using his telekinetic powers.

"Tommy!" Dr. Vasence bellowed as he neared him. "How goes it?"

"Okay. Kinda' swamped." Tommy shifted his weight from one leg to the other. He was actually bored.

"Mind helping these nice people out with some food?"

"Sure, not at all. Just tell me what you need."

He directed this to the small parade and frowned as most of them backed up in fright.

The female reporter mustered up a little courage and stepped closer to him.

"So, Tommy, how long have you been here?"

"About twelve years."

"Really? Does it bother you that your parents abandoned you?"

"Not really, I have my brothers here with me."

That seemed to shock her and she reared back a bit.

"Your brothers?"

"Yeah, we all came together. I was like not quite five, my younger brother was three and the little guy was ten months."

"Your parents just gave up all of you based on a test? That's terrible."

"Is it? I wouldn't have thought so by the rate these kids come through here every month."

"Tommy can be very opinionated,"

Professor Graham said narrowing his eyes.

Tommy turned away to check on his burgers. He hated working the kitchen but it kept him preoccupied. His rival, Janti, who at that very moment was staring at him from across the room, gave him a smirk. They made their contact brief before anyone noticed. Everyone in this facility had secrets.

～

Professor Makoto stood at the panoramic window in his office overlooking Tokyo and took in the new landscape. Large barriers invisible to the naked eye at ground level surrounded the island to combat future tsunamis and a structure was erected beneath to prevent sinking. It was all in preparation for the ship sitting at the bottom of the Pacific Ocean to rise out. He was not taking any chances for another disaster to set his country back and it wasn't just Japan. His authority spanned most of Asia.

New advances in architecture and technology were discovered then utilized at every turn. Much of it stemmed from the wounded alien the Americans had captured, kept under lock and key, decades ago. Of course, Japan had their own captive but Professor Makoto kept that secret from his colleagues. He knew the pact they made in the beginning when the ships crashed would not hold water. The first thing Professor Lancaster did was isolate the one he found and denied access to any data derived from communicating with the alien.

What he did find grateful was the joint data regarding the children born with extraordinary capabilities. There was such an array of different combinations, his team almost couldn't keep up. In the country side fifty miles between Osaka and Nagoya a small facility housed them. He liked to think the children were being cared for exceptionally well but he knew there was always going to be workers who feared and harmed them. That couldn't be helped.

"Professor Makoto?"

A male aide peeked his head into the doorway,

waiting patiently for permission to enter. He was young, just barely twenty and one of the half breed children. His hair was naturally light brown hanging past his shoulder in slight waves. Dark green eyes set amid oriental features blinked back at him.

"Come in, Hana." He watched the young man blush at the cruel name that suited his exceptional beauty. "What have you got for me today?"

"Umm, Dr. Kiroshi wants to know if he can release one of the special soldiers for duty. There seems to be a skirmish in one of Hokkaido's outer regions."

"Rebel military, again?"

A few factions seemed to think the government shouldn't use half aliens in the military because of the clear advantage it gave. They had no idea it was the scientific community, not the government, running the military these days.

"He believes so, yes." Hana had a soft docile voice.

Professor Makoto turned away from his sprawling view of Tokyo and walked towards him, stopping within a few feet.

"Permission granted." A few strands of hair fell in front of Hana's face and the Professor used a finger to move them back behind his ear. "Would you indulge an old man and have dinner with me this evening?"

"Uh, of course, sir. May I ask why?"

"I think we should get to know more about each other if we're going to work so closely from now on. Don't you think?"

"Yes, that sounds reasonable." Hana gripped his notepad close to his body with both hands. "I will let Dr. Kiroshi know about your decision right away." He turned to leave, his hand almost at the door handle.

"Oh, and Hana," Professor Makoto began, "Please come in female stage and wear a dress." He watched

Hana's hand shake a little as it paused on the handle.

"Yes, sir."

"Don't be nervous, Hana. I am not going to harm you. Please do not take me for those animals who hurt you in the facility."

"Of course not, sir. I'm sorry." His hand relaxed. "I look forward to dinner, sir."

As Hana left, Professor Makoto sighed. It angered him, the lack of trust still lingering among the older ones. He had heard some of the horror stories coming out of other facilities and refused to let such things happen on his watch. They may not be prevented entirely but they could be contained. More thorough education for the workers was key. Turning back to his view, he decided to pay a visit to his facility within the month.

◠

The head engineer spoke into his headset connecting him with the engineering crews worldwide.

"How are we looking boys?"

Every engineer on hand was called in for a routine check on the reinforced cities infrastructure surrounding the crash sites. Small reverberations shook the ground signaling the activation of the ships' systems. To lift out of their temporary prisons, the ships would cause another massive wave of earthquakes except this time with minimal damage. For the first time, the general public would get to see them in detail, a stark contrast from the fiery balls of death over fifty years ago.

"I want a twenty-four-hour watch on those monstrosities when they come up for air."

When he was first assigned to his job, it was a massive top-secret undertaking. As a team, his colleagues fostered hundreds of ideas on how to prevent devastation in the wake of a scenario such as this. In the end, they went with area specific resolutions. It still boggled his mind that aliens had crash landed on Earth in his lifetime. The twenty first century was looking more and more like something out of a Sci-Fi movie.

"Check the feed, sir. I think we're good to go." The voice in his ear interrupted his thoughts. "Just have to sit and wait now."

"Sounds like it won't be long." He could feel tingles in his feet from the low rumble beneath and watched the coffee in his mug form ripples.

"Those scientists have some crazy timing."

Feeling the ground shake about a year before, the scientists in charge decided to let the world in on what really happened and its outcome. They assumed giving advanced warning meant there would be no surprise at the ships' reveal. He could attest they were wrong on that front. There would be panic, riots and all out terror.

"Yep, wait and see," he replied to no one, heading back to the viewing bunker.

⌒

Captain Darnizva stood once again at the helm of his ship overseeing preparations to engage the secondary engines for ascension from the deep, cavernous underground. His uniform was like second skin compared to the clothes he wore during his infiltration. He leaned over the bar of the raised dais and set his weight down on it.

His red robe brushed against the floor. Every high ranked officer had their own style of uniform and Darnizva had gone with simplicity. Black leggings and boots, white tunic, and red cloak fastened at the waist with a black sash. All worn to accentuate his dark wavy hair and cinnamon red eyes.

After forty years of exploring the planet, he went back to his fighter vessel and traveled beneath the surface to his ship. In the past ten years, he was able to establish communication with the other downed ships and relay the information he had collected. By travelling unseen underground, they found some useful resources to repair much of the damage. Even some of his crew were more willing to venture out and explore Earth.

He had fathered two children from two women of different generations. The first was already in his forties, married with three children of his own and the other just finished his Master's Degree in Information Technology. Upon finding out his origin, his first mate was, in her own words, 'freaked the fuck out'. Yet, the second seemed surprisingly comfortable with it since she herself was a hybrid offspring. Thinking about his sons and grandchildren gave him a sense of accomplishment.

To prepare his crew for the inhabitants of Earth in the Americas sector, he spoke in the human English language. His crew still had trouble, citing its difficulty to learn. With words jumbled often and out of context, a new translation device was manufactured to give them an advantage.

"How long before we can lift off?" He asked his navigator.

"T.D….A.T…ETD thirty-six hours, Captain." The navigator frowned in frustration.

"Very good."

He heard the bridge door open and his second in command hurried in to take his seat next to the navigator. Captain Darnizva watched him get to his tasks and wondered what the soldier was thinking. He had forgiven him for the jettison out of the ship to save his life but it seemed to be a non-issue for him. Darnizva still considered his actions were unwarranted.

"We're going to use the rotation blades to lessen the damage. This way the broken ground will fill up beneath us as we ascend."

"That is the plan, sir. Are we coordinating with the others?"

"Of course. Might as well introduce ourselves in one shot."

WARM WELCOMES

In Italy, the city of Terni shook with angry vigor as the alien ship buried deep below slowly made its way back to the surface. The newly built infrastructures were kept from collapsing but not from swaying. Anything not bolted down was tossed around and windows shattered from the vibrations. Citizens not trusting the new designs' ability to withstand the onslaught were evacuated into underground bunkers where they stayed while the quakes went on for hours.

By early dawn the next day, the tremors ceased and a massive ship sat above ground humming softly. Its vibrations made the air shimmer in waves like summer heat. Already, there were camera crews, a large gathering of civilians and military personnel surrounding it waiting, watching.

The soldiers were there mostly for crowd control, not anticipating any hostile behavior from the aliens per Professor Morandi's instructions. As a precaution, weapons were locked and loaded. A loud reverberation emitted from the ship and everyone present stood awe-struck as a ramp protruded from the open landing dock. It settled onto the ground with a resounding thunder.

"Look! They're coming out!" A man from the crowd shouted.

Cameras zoomed in on the five figures walking down in perfect unison, their features made visible as they got closer. The one in front was a male dressed in a deep purple full body suit with black boots and a black cloak fasten at the waist. Even from a distance, his eyes glowed the color of dark lavender. Jet black hair held at bay by a purple bandana fell past his shoulders. He resembled a samurai from the Edo period. Four other males flanked him, two on each side wearing all black and what appeared to be weapons strapped to their right thighs. The five halted their procession when their boots touched solid earth.

A government agent pushed the scared and nervous Italian representative forward and angrily gestured for him to advance. He gulped loudly and motioned for his entourage to join him. All six eventually made their way slowly behind him. Within a hundred yards from the aliens, they stopped.

"Ehh, Good morning. How are you? I am Gioberto Torini." Torini could hear his own voice shaking and blew out a big puff of air to calm his nerves.

A holoscreen appeared in midair before the alien leader and strange characters moved around on it before rearranging into groups resembling words. There was an eerie silence as all five aliens focused their attention on it. The leader looked towards the crowd.

"Good morning. I am Lieutenant Zanzibar."

His Italian was perfect.

Sharp intakes of breath were heard throughout the crowd. Torini sighed in relief that he wasn't killed on the spot. Feeling a little better, he continued his questions.

"Are you the leader of your race?"

"No, I am a soldier. This is my battleship." He swept a hand in front of the other four. "These are my personal guards."

MAQUEL A. JACOB

"What planet do you come from?"

"Our planet is called Karysilan. It is quite far away, but within your galaxy." Zanzibar touched the holoscreen and a virtual map of the world appeared. It zoomed in on a pinpointed area. "This place, where we stand, it is called Italy?"

"Yes, that's correct."

"And we are speaking this regions language?"

"Yes." Torini felt the harsh stares from the crowd for his short responses. He didn't know what they wanted him to do or ask of the aliens. A light bulb turned on in his mind and he made a bold suggestion. "Would you like a tour of our city?"

Zanzibar glanced at his guards. The one in back on his right opened his mouth as a tiny probe extended from behind his ear to curve in front of him. A speech unlike anything humans had ever heard flowed from his lips. Loud guttural tones with an electronic tinge to it. When he was finished, the tiny probe retracted back behind the ear and inside his head.

"That would be appreciated."

"You seem to have a pretty good grasp of our language," Torini laughed nervously.

"Our system was able to do a thorough analysis." The holoscreen disappeared.

"Will your crew be alright?"

"Of course."

"By the way, how many soldiers are on your ship?"

"Three thousand."

Torini visibly blanched. He turned to the government agents for help and received blanked stares. They too were shocked by the number. Looking at the size of the ship, he should have known there would be a lot of them. His nervousness intensified as the aliens got close enough to touch and he had to look up at them. He calculated Zanzibar at

122

a solid six feet eight inches tall and his guards were two to three inches taller than him. The crowd gasped.

"Is there a problem?" Zanzibar asked.

His eyes scanned the area, noticing the armed soldiers surrounding his ship.

"No, no, no!" Torini insisted. "It's just that, you are quite tall."

"Are there not humans our height?"

"Well, yes. But, it is not common."

"And the ones with weapons?"

"Just a precaution," Torini laughed again, wiping sweat from his brow with a handkerchief his assistant passed to him. "Are you hungry?"

"We would like to try your form of sustenance. I understand food varies by continent on this planet."

"Yes, yes, but Italian food is the best." This Torini said with pride and conviction.

"Please, lead the way."

Professor Morandi watched the scene transpire from the safety of her bunker and nodded with approval. Her instructions were to treat the aliens as if nothing was out of the ordinary. Just some visitors dropping by for a little vacation which turned out to be the right call. She knew they would not be hostile. The same protocol was to be implemented with the other ships. A new dawn had risen for mankind with the hybrid children, but now a second one was underway.

Observing Zanzibar, she made note of his demeanor. He was not to be toyed with. It was plain to see that he would not let himself or his crew be taken captive. The other factor she became aware of dealt with why their ships crashed in the first place. Her eyes narrowed in thought.

Where Italy showed hospitality, the Prime Minister of Russia was not about to be so cordial despite the list of protocol instructions. There were a handful of civilians, four government officials and a military troop of one hundred ready for combat. He stood legs apart, arms down at his sides as the ship's ramp lower to the ground. A nod from the commanding officer sent the soldiers into a semicircle formation around the ship. It took a lot of advanced coordination considering its size. He braced himself for the encounter.

A female in a white romper style leotard with white boots and a light green cloak fastened with a white sash at the waist marched out of the ship flanked by two other females and two males. The two females wore the white leotards sans cloak and the males were in full body suits, weapons strapped to their thighs.

"Be ready to engage if necessary," the commanding officer whispered into his wrist communicator.

"Cancel that order, soldier," Professor Pretchov hissed over the commlink. "If you so much as cock a chamber, I will make sure you meet your maker sooner than later."

"Begging your pardon, Doctor," the officer snapped, "but I will not let some alien hostiles annihilate our country, or the human race for that matter."

"They are not hostile unless you become a threat. Stand down and follow protocol!"

All the anxiety drained from the Prime Minister's body as he got a clear visual on the females, especially the leader. Her hair, a mixture of white, pink and sea foam green cascaded down past her hips. Eyes the same green as her cloak shone brightly and her full lips spread into a soft smile.

He watched the well-toned thigh muscles work as she walked and didn't realize how close her entourage had come until he had to look up from his perfect view of her abdomen.

"My Gods!" He exclaimed staring up at her.

She was nearly seven feet tall, the others a few inches shorter, though still impressive.

"Hmm? I think not," she said sweetly. "I am no one's God."

"You speak Russian?" He asked incredulous.

"I listened from before and learned. I was told it is a very hard language but I found it quite easy."

She smiled wide and the Prime Minister fell in love, mentally begging his wife's forgiveness.

The commanding officer lowered his weapon having the same sentiment, also mesmerized by the stunning female leader's thigh muscles. Her two female guards weren't too shabby either.

They could crack a man's ribs.

No animals made their presence known in the deep forest, holding an eerie silence. The strange humming caused the vegetation and trees to shiver softly in an invisible wind tunnel. In its center sat an alien ship nearly a mile in diameter surrounded by American soldiers ready and willing to open fire if whatever came out was perceived as remotely hostile. Yes, it went against the protocol but better safe than sorry.

General Hoskins had personally come to the crash site to bear witness to the historic event. No question their race and the planet would evolve going forward. Turning to Secretary of Defense Eileen Regis, he cleared his throat.

"So, Madam Secretary, what do you think of our predecessors' decision to let the scientists handle this?"

"Asinine." Regis shook her head slightly as she replied. "But, on the other hand, we may not have gotten this far if we hadn't agreed.

"You may be right." Hoskins let out a deep breath and puffed up his chest. "Well, let's see what we've gotten ourselves into. Here they come."

From high above, a long vertical strip of the hull appeared and parted in the center. The lower section came down creating a ramp and out of the gaping darkness five figures appeared. As they descended towards the group of media, military, and politicians, Regis eyed General Hoskins making note of the aliens' attire with more scrutiny towards the body armor and weapons strapped to their thighs which she too found intriguing. The four flanking the leader were in all black body suits with shiny metal covering the forearms, chest and knees. All of them had hair of the same color but their eyes shone brilliant shades of blue.

Their leader was dressed entirely different wearing red, black and white. His hair was not as dark and his eyes were the cinnamon red of a demon. The slight smirk on the alien's face was a tad creepy. Fastened at the waist, the red cloak flowed behind him like a superhero, his black boots striking the ramp surface with just enough force to echo.

General Hoskins made a signal with his fingers alerting the soldiers to be ready and stopped midway when the alien leader raised a finger himself and wagged it while shaking his head. The General went visibly pale and dared not look at Secretary Regis to let her see the terror in his eyes. But, she had already sensed something amiss with the General. Stepping forward along with four armed guards she went to greet the leader, her assistants joining behind. She pursed her lips in disgust at the lack of resolve on the General's part.

As usual, it takes a woman to get the job done, she thought to herself.

"Welcome to Earth, visitor. I am not sure if you understand me, but…" She saw his hand go up to stop her speech.

"I understand you very well, Madam Secretary of Defense. It is good to meet you." A sly smile crept on his face and she knew he was enjoying the shocked looks on all their faces.

"It seems you have done your homework. May I ask what you go by?"

"I am Captain Darnizva of the League from planet Karysilan. During my adventures on Earth, I went by David."

"Your adventures…?" Regis started, then thought better of it. He was taunting her; she was sure of it. "And, how did you enjoy your sightseeing?"

"Very amusing." Darnizva cocked his head to one side as he stared past her.

Secretary Regis was puzzled by his answer until she followed his line of sight. Her heart rate shot up at the small group of soldiers positioning themselves closer in the trees. Keep the conversation going! She yelled at herself internally. Panic was not an option.

"Well, we do aim to please. Where exactly did you travel?"

"Oh," Darnizva began, switching his glance to her yet not moving his head from its cocked position, "England was first, then Canada and finally the United States."

Regis waved a hand to one of her assistants and pointed to the General who still stood in a state of fear, erect like a statue. Without speaking a word, she relayed what she wanted. Her assistants were fluent in her mannerisms from observing everything she did. Thus, she knew they had also seen the small sniper unit creeping up in the trees. Her number two female assistant turned sharply and marched up to the General. Heated words were exchanged.

"How is that possible when your ship landed here in the U.S.?"

"My second in command thought saving my life took precedence over all things and sent me out in a combat fighter."

"Surely you praised him." She smiled.

"No. Selfish acts of desperation are not tolerated." The response was like a knife making her rear back in surprise. "Of course, I had to forgive him. He is my second in command and I need him."

"I assume you know, then, that the president would like to speak with you along with other affluent members of our country?"

"Hmm. Before that, Madam Secretary, we must deal with that."

His gaze shifted back to the snipers and tilting his head back upright, lifted one finger in the air.

The two alien guards in the back stepped out of formation and raised their right arms. A tiny probe protruded out from behind their ears and harsh electronic guttural speech emitted from their mouths. Their arms reconfigured, the hands going into the arm and a hollow opening took its place. The holes widened then solidified, transforming into mini cannons with blue light glowing from within.

Secretary Regis eyes nearly bulged out of their sockets as the cannons fired without making a sound. The rounds hit the trees with bone crunching, cracking sounds filling the air as partly disintegrated trees came down one by one. Both guards moved the cannons in short precise movements targeting each sniper's location.

With nothing below them now, the snipers plummeted to the ground. The alien guards in the front raised their arms when the soldiers were thirty feet from their deaths and an intricate web of light burst forward forming a net beneath them. It slowly fell to the ground, the soldiers safely landed before it disappeared.

"No more of that, don't you think?" Darnizva quipped.

Composing herself once again, Secretary Regis held her head up high and straightened her dress uniform jacket.

"I assure you, this is not our protocol procedure. This was to be a peaceful interaction."

"Oh, I know. I received reports from the other ships. I believe your head of command was being overly cautious."

"General Hoskins is not confident that your agenda is peaceful."

"Well, believe me when I tell you, Earth was not our destination. It was a random coordinate." Darnizva walked the rest of the way down the ramp and stepped closer to tower over her. "I did not get your name, Madam Secretary."

"My apologies, my name is Eileen Regis."

"A pleasure to meet you," Darnizva held out his hand and she shook it. "Now, how about a tour of this sector of the country?"

"But you've seen it already, if I recall."

"Yes, but my crew has not. I think if we took maybe twenty or thirty at a time each day that would not be too much of a burden."

"Surely, you're joking?" She laughed.

"No," he replied, "I am not."

"But, why?"

"Because, Madam Secretary, the more we familiarize

ourselves with your planet and ways of life, the better we can defend it."

"Defend?" She did not like the sound of what was coming.

"It may be best to discuss these matters with your president first."

Feeling the color drain out of her, Regis nodded. She was no tactician but concluded as much. If Earth was not their destination, and it needed defending, that meant they were being chased by another race. Possibly one far more formidable than the Karysilans. Fate was a cruel mistress indeed. Gesturing towards the media group, she resumed her role of ambassador and escorted Darnizva with guards in tow, out of the forest.

RECON

Over the course of six months, people opposed to the presence of Bi-Genetic humans came out of the shadows in force but found their voices combating the opinions of the masses. Even some factions of the LGBT community, known for its tolerance of others, came out against the new species. They were seen not only as alien by-products, but not falling in the category of gay or lesbian since they assumed all Bi-Genetics could just choose a gender.

Aliens travelling to different countries, learning each culture, were surprised by the onslaught of prejudice and hatred. It was not something they understood. Vitriol was rampant in the United States.

Professor Lancaster didn't know how much more he could take. It seemed like the world had slid backwards instead of leaping forward. A chance arose to have a sit down with a small group visiting from the Russia ship so he decided to pick their brains. He chose a restaurant located on the forty second floor of a prominent hotel with a sprawling view of the city at midday.

They sat at a table close to the window enjoying a staple business meal; Steak with all the fixings. Professor Lancaster watched the four extremely tall soldiers take small attentive bites to ensure they tasted every flavor. It still fascinated him that these aliens were of a similar carbon base like humans yet so very different.

"Why is there such strife among your own people?"

The seemingly young soldier asked abruptly after he finished chewing. The group had researched an article on restaurant etiquette before ordering.

"Don't you have factions in your system who pit themselves against authority or issues that are not deemed beneficial to society?" Lancaster asked.

"Of course, but we do not wage war against ourselves. Our enemies manifest in other races from different planets."

"But, you have people of different," Professor Lancaster struggled for the right word, "attributes, like skin color, eye color and so forth."

"Yes. But, what does that have to do with anything? We are all Karysilan."

Professor Lancaster was speechless. Compared to them Humans were primitive, petty and weak minded. He began to think his race was undeserving to be defended by them. Organizations for world peace had been saying that very thing for as long as he could remember and now aliens were making the case.

"And," the soldier next to him added, "Why is there such an uproar over our offspring?"

"Well, because some of them are capable of changing their gender."

"So? It is the nature of a species to adapt to the situation when necessary. Many of our warriors are taken out of battle to raise children and learn civilian ways of life to understand why we defend our kind."

"Is that so?" Professor Lancaster sat up straighter.

"When you find a mate, it is only a matter of time before you decide to procreate."

"I am quite humbled. I just wish our race had the same sentiment."

"Since it is a new era of your kind, it may take some time."

"But, that is not something we have if what your Captain Darnizva hinted at is true."

The four soldiers glanced at each other and did not respond. That was answer enough for Professor Lancaster. A televised discussion was scheduled at the Captain's discretion but a specific time had not been announced yet. He wondered what the wait was for and knew he would have his answer soon.

⌒

"Oh, Dear God!" Talley Crohm, the observations head, exclaimed as he stood up staring wide eyed at the monitor showing a live feed of space.

Just outside Mar's orbit, the darkness sucked inward on itself and a whirling tunnel opened wide to spew out a Karysilan battle ship, its mass much larger than the ones that crashed on Earth. Calculations came flooding in on its trajectory and diameter, scrambling personnel to assess possible damage if it too decided to land.

General Hoskins, fully recovered from his embarrassment six months ago, came barging into the center to see what the ruckus was all about. He had been assigned to the underground bunker as a punishment but now saw it as a blessing. On the observation deck, he took command.

"What's its ETA?" He barked at Talley.

Talley snapped his fingers at the man below him and was greeted with wild eyes. "Give it to me!" He watched the man's fingers fly across the keyboard and then stop. Talley leaned over the bar separating them and quickly scanned the data. "Twenty-six hours, sir! It's moving hella fast!"

"How big is it?"

"Oh, I'd say about twelve miles in diameter," Talley replied with a hint of sarcasm.

"Is that thing going to try and land?" General Hoskins exploded.

"I certainly hope not, sir."

"Mercy on all of us," he muttered.

∽

Captain Darnizva sat patiently in the oval office with the President of the United States and most of his advisors. The news about another ship coming down spear headed a massive rush for emergency procedures and possible evacuation. He was there to quell their fears but he couldn't help watching the humans run around a bit, quite amused by their determination. When it was clear the situation was getting out of hand, he loudly cleared his throat, getting the attention of everyone.

"Ladies." He nodded to the females in the room. "Gentlemen. There is no need to panic. That ship is not landing. It will dock just outside Earth's orbit and a convoy ship will be sent down."

The vice president spun on him red faced.

"Why didn't you tell us that before we went through all of this?"

A hushed silence filled the room and Darnizva saw the realization on the man's face that he had just yelled at an alien who could kill them all in one motion.

"It would have been good to know, is what I'm saying," he added in a muted tone.

"Because, it was hilarious," Darnizva laughed. "Do you always run amuck into action without first asking questions or assessing the situation?"

Everyone glanced away from each other in humiliation. They had all failed tactics 101 and in the face of a higher being. President Pulham moved over to his desk and leaned back against it, shoving his hands in his pants pockets.

"Who is it that's coming, Captain?"

"My father, General Phalkar, and the rest of the League's high-ranking officers."

The President nodded twice and looked up at the ceiling. "Why is he coming?"

"As I said, we may need to defend this planet, and although I am also a high-ranking officer, I do not have that authority."

"Will you be explaining the situation, then, when they get here?"

"That is the plan, Mr. President. Is there a venue big enough for the convoy ship to land?"

Secretary Regis tapped her lower lip. "How big is the ship?"

"Perhaps about a fifth of a football field."

"Then, we can use a football field. One with a covered dome. We don't need fly over spectators."

"But, you are going to have media outlets?"

"That's different," the White House Press Secretary interjected. "We are going to have them contained within the dome along with our other guests."

"Other guests?" Darnizva's eyebrows shot upward.

"Dignitaries, military and such," the Vice President said.

"Get it done." President Pulham had spoken.

While people rushed to the task at hand Darnizva and his guards remained. He knew the President wanted to speak with him alone by the way he stayed leaning against his desk in reverie. Finally, he moved away from it and stood in front of Darnizva.

"Are we talking world ending calamity or just mass devastation?"

"Hard to say. We never really know what our enemy

is thinking half the time. If they deem this planet not worth their time, it may just be mass devastation. If some other factor comes into play, then…" Darnizva stopped.

"Then what?"

"Invasion. They take control of your planet. Or, they destroy it."

"Great." President Pulham turned away and walked to his office window. "Who is this enemy of yours?"

"They are called Relliants and are something quite vicious. You have a term here called sleeper cells, yes?"

President turned to him, his mouth dropped.

"Why would you ask that?"

"Did it never occur to your scientists that a few of their ships may have gotten caught up in our jump and crash landed here?"

The President's posture faltered and he barely made it into his chair, holding his head with both hands. It may have been an information overload after all. Darnizva got up and went to lean over the President's desk, forcing the man to make eye contact. Orbs of blue clouded with despair stared back at him.

"Mr. President, your country is not the only one affected by this dilemma. The reason I chose to have the discussion here is because of your country's status in the world. A new dawn of humankind is about to explode and you all need to find a common ground." The President sat up and his expression changed from despair to intrigue. "I fear your kind will falter far more than it should before realizing it's too late."

"We are a divided race," the President stated.

"Full of prejudice, envy and hate for one another," Darnizva finished for him.

"There may not be any hope for us."

"You can at least try. No race has ever changed without trying."

Five jet fighters escorted the alien convoy ship to the domed arena outside the city. Air traffic control designated the tristate areas as no-fly zones to eliminate collisions or onlookers. The night sky was void of clouds giving flight command an unobstructed view of their approach. At the ten-mile mark, the dome opened three quarters of the way allowing the convoy ship quick entry as it positioned itself above. While it descended, the dome proceeded with a fast closure. The fighter jets took off to land in the emptied parking lot converted to a landing sight.

Inside the arena, one section of the stands was filled with dignitaries and military while the other side in stark contrast was crammed with media groups. This news development appeared to be better fodder than the Bi-Genetic facilities or the ships emergence. A platform was set up on the field in front of an empty section so the scientists and technicians with the authority to demand it could have front row viewing.

Hot blasts of wind whipped through the stadium pushing people backwards, tumbling equipment and anything else not secured up into the air. Cameramen held on to their gear for dear life while the dignitaries tried to shield themselves from the onslaught. Military personnel just sat back and took it. That was nothing, especially for those who had seen combat. The wind died down as the convoy ship settled down next to the platform. Overhead lights switched on signaling the closure of the dome and silence ensued.

Loud humming erupted from the craft when opened. A ramp extended, slamming to the ground and embedding in the turf. Waves of heat shimmered in the air preventing the audience from deciphering the figures coming out until they were halfway down. From the bleacher section, Captain Darnizva and Lieutenant

Zanzibar made their way to join them.

The first two who came down were striking, almost blinding. In what appeared to be a body suit of starlight, a silver haired male oozing arrogance, sashayed to the edge of the ramp. His silver colored eyes glinted mischievously. The female was full figured in an all-white leotard, boots and robe fastened at the waist. Her hair was jet black as were her irises, yet she was stunningly beautiful.

Behind them were two males of equal massive size and obvious authority. The male on the left had hair and eyes of gold. His body suit white with gold boots and robe to accent it. Secured on his sash by a large hoop was a three-foot-long golden battle axe. To his right was the most formidable creature any human in the room had encountered. Hair the color of fresh blood shimmering with fire cascaded down past his shoulders onto an equally red robe. He wore a black body suit with red boots. His eyes, as red as his hair, were what frightened them all.

"Is that a demon?" A reporter whispered to the one next to him. The other man's wild eyes turned on him and he just shook his head. "We're fucking screwed."

Captain Darnizva and Lt. Zanzibar took their place behind the first two as the entourage halted on the grassy knoll. Clicks from cameras echoed in continuous succession from the media section. The President of the United States took the lead and stood to speak.

"Welcome to Earth. I am President Pulham, of the United States. I do not speak for the entire human race so those who speak for their countries are here in attendance If it is not too much to ask, can you introduce yourselves so we know who we are addressing."

"Mmm, quite bold, isn't he?" The one of starlight turned, asking Darnizva. Looking back at the President, he answered.

"I am Lieutenant Sspark and wielder of the Sphere."

He saw Darnizva roll his eyes upward.

"I am Commander Ammordia," the beauty in white cut in. "Please forgive the Lieutenant. He is unaware that you have no idea what he is referring to." She smiled pleasantly and bowed. Sspark's eyes narrowed but she continued. "Behind me is Admiral Goulld." Her outstretched arm moved towards the one in gold. "And, this is our General, Phalkar." She gestured towards the red demon standing in silence, staring straight ahead at the scientists on the platform who were visibly shaken.

"That's his father?" One of the American Generals whispered, too scared to speak any louder than that to his colleague beside him.

"Christ, I thought the son was creepy," his colleague whispered back.

The President let out a heavy sigh to calm his nerves and continued the session, noticing the audience starting to clamor for the information they came for. At that moment, he realized there may be panic or a riot and felt guilty for not preparing for the worst sooner.

"Captain Darnizva has stated that a threat may present itself to our planet and has asked that we get your permission to help us defend it. Can you please clarify this?"

The President sat down in his seat shaking uncontrollably. Secretary Regis squeezed his hand, calming him down a bit.

"There is a war going on between our race and one called the Relliants," Ammordia began. "It has been going on for quite some time off and on spanning centuries. It took a devastating toll on both sides this time around and our front line fled to save lives. I am sure you noticed the other seven ships spread across your solar system." There were gasps at this revelation but she continued.

"Unfortunately, that jump put them near an inhabited planet with no way of stopping their crash landing due to the massive damage incurred." She halted her story a moment to let it sink in so far. When the din of raised voices died out, she finished. "There may have been a few Relliant ships caught up in the jump who also crashed and now reside on your planet. Because of these ill-fated circumstances, we are obliged to assist."

"How long do we have before they come looking to continue this fight?"

The President had recovered somewhat.

"Possibly fifty years, give or take. It depends on when the ones on Earth reveal themselves."

Some sighs of relief could be heard from the dignitary section and there was clear appall for it, making the culprits suddenly feel like targets. Darnizva stepped forward and stared up at them.

"Are you content that it will not be in your lifetime? Do you think it is wise for you to condemn your countries to death without trying to find a remedy? I ask you this. Do you think your current technology, or any that you develop on your own will adequately defend this planet?"

He turned to the President and bore his stare into his.

"You think I don't know you have some of our warriors hidden in bunkers for your own sick experiments? That your advanced infrastructure came from their knowledge? I will tell you, that knowledge alone is not enough. They know very little compared to the many races out in the universe."

The President went pale and turned to the Secretary of Defense, then to Professor Lancaster who shied away from his glance. He ran his hand down his face and squeezed his eyes shut for a moment. He had no idea, and now he was angry. Plausible deniability was not going to cut it this time. He should have been told. Looking back at General Phalkar, he now had a clue as to why the demon's glare never wavered from the scientists.

"We will now open the floor for questions from the media," the Press Secretary announced.

Hands shot up immediately and he had a hard time choosing who would be first. He decided to choose the reporter from France.

"You."

"So, to verify. We have only fifty years, maybe, to advance our technology and be on par with yours in order to defend ourselves?"

"That is correct," Ammordia replied. Exclamations around the dome grew.

"Next, the one in the yellow tie." The Press Secretary pointed to another foreign reporter.

"Are we talking about space combat? No ground troops?"

"It would be ideal to keep them at bay in space but I'm afraid your ground troops will need to be trained in hand to hand combat."

"We know all about hand to hand combat," a German General snapped, obviously offended.

"Oh?" Sspark shifted his weight from one leg to the other. "You've fought an advanced alien race's warrior clan before?"

That led to another bout of silence as every human in the dome understood the weight of his words like a two-ton heavy thing. Their planet's military arrogance would get them annihilated. Fifty years was not enough time.

"Who would be teaching us these new combat maneuvers?" General Hoskins asked.

"That would be us, of course, but mainly I," Sspark replied smiling.

Darnizva stood akimbo and nodded to the human guards at the stadium entrance near the platform. As they left, he held his head a little higher.

"A demonstration, perhaps?"

"What?" The President sat up straight, incredulous. "What is he talking about?"

General Hoskins leaned forward in his seat so the President could see him.

"We took the liberty to find some of our most hardened and ferocious prisoners for this demonstration."

"Say what?" The President yelled.

"Calm down, sir. These are terrorist, murderers, you name it. They jumped at a chance to go head to head with these aliens."

"Have you lost your mind?" The President seethed. "Who authorized this?"

"The scientists' votes were unanimous. They want to see this more than anyone."

The President glared over at the scientists' section and a few of them shrugged then smirked. He was not amused. An unpleasantness came over him as the first prisoner was led in by two armed soldiers. His stomach lurched and he became woozy. A glance at the media cameras zooming in solidified his unrest.

The prisoner's restraints were removed and he walked into the center, staring down the alien group, daring one of them to come at him. Sspark laughed.

"He's ready to go, isn't he?" Sspark walked down to the edge of the platform. "I will show you what it means to be the wielder of a sphere."

Holding out one hand, a small orb of light formed, growing to grapefruit size. It then elongated into a six-foot rod and solidified. Sspark spun it with deadly force and in the blink of an eye was a good fifty feet in the air, coming down fast on the prisoner. There was no time for the man to react and he was hit with enough force to knock his body face down flat, making a dent in the platform. Sspark had arched his body backwards the moment he struck and was back in the air. He landed softly on tiptoes where he started, a proud look on his face. Not a bead of sweat or signs of exertion visible, as if he'd done nothing.

"Do you have a better one? This one was no fun at all."

He tossed the long metal stick in front of him and it reverted to a glowing orb, disappearing in his hand as he caught it.

All eyes were on the prisoner still embedded in the floor. Everything had happened in mere seconds. The best fighter on the planet could not do such a thing. Every General and world leader in attendance realized just how inadequate their current military was.

Two more soldiers came from the walkway to retrieve the body. A black tarp was thrown over him and he was rolled into it in such a way so no one could see how the front of the body fared. As it was swiftly carried out, sounds of vomiting came from various sections of the dome. It took everything the President had to not follow suit as another prisoner was ushered in. This one also too eager and raring to go.

"Come on! Let's break some shit!" The six feet five bald, tattooed mass of muscle exploded. He paced the floor waiting for one of the League officers to approach. The President recognized him. One of the most feared terrorists of their time. A glory killer with no discrimination for his prey: A butcher of men, women and children. A child rapist, gun runner and assassin for hire. Even so, there was an odd sense of pity.

"Is he fucking stupid?" A well renowned female journalist exclaimed turning from one colleague to another. They just shook their heads. "What person in their right mind would go up against an alien and think they can win?"

"The ones who've seen too many Sci-Fi movies where we always win," a colleague replied.

"I have a bad feeling about this one," another one added.

Zanzibar stepped up onto the platform and with slow, precise movements removed the long sword from his waist, setting it down behind him.

"Oh! You think you don't need that, huh? Wanna' go head to head!"

The prisoner inhaled deeply, puffing up his chest, then let out a primal yell. He positioned himself in a boxer's stance and made a few practice jabs.

"Lieutenant," Ammordia spoke. Zanzibar glanced back at her. "Be gentle. Let's not scare them any more than necessary." He nodded in acknowledgement.

The prisoner bounced around and thumbing his nose, sniffed. His eyes went wide as he flew backwards, landing on his tailbone at the opposite side of the platform. Zanzibar now stood a few inches from where the prisoner once did. His posture made it seem like he had not moved, his speed undetected. Angry, the prisoner rigorously shook his head and jumped up.

"It's on now!"

He advanced towards Zanzibar and switched to a combination of mixed martial art maneuvers. Zanzibar matched his speed effortlessly never veering from his inner sanctum giving the illusion of standing still. The prisoner tried to get a hit but to no avail. It was as if Zanzibar had an invisible wall around him.

"Oh, really Lieutenant!" Sspark said, exasperated. "Finish it."

Blurred lines formed around the prisoner and with them, thin tendrils of blood. Zanzibar landed blows at a speed no one could see. Not even the last one that sent the prisoner through the air and embedding the wall above the walkway. So deep in was his body that it did not fall. A spiral design of blood covered the platform. Zanzibar walked over, retrieved his sword and attached it to his waist. He returned to his place with the other officers.

Sspark clapped mockingly and received a look of disapproval from Ammordia. He stopped and glanced around at the horrified faces of the humans which made him laugh a little before he thought better of it, regaining a straight face. Darnizva squared his shoulders and turned away from the body in the wall.

"Enough!" President Pulham yelled. "No more demonstrations! We get it!"

"Do you?" The voice was deep, booming and raised the hair on every human's body. This was the first time the demon General had spoken and they all wished he hadn't. "We are holding back. If this were a true battle..." he stopped speaking and his eyes burned redder, piercing souls.

"We will take your guidance," Professor Makoto announced. His colleagues, as well as he, knew their current technology and skills were nowhere near the level of defending Earth. Every nation needed to cooperate to pull that off.

"Good."

General Phalkar turned as did the other officers and walked back towards their convoy ship.

"Did you not want to take a tour of the city?" The Press Secretary suggested.

"Have you gone mad?" General Hoskins hissed through gritted teeth at him.

The Press Secretary realized what he had just asked and saw the looks of terror on every man and woman's face.

So stupid! He chided himself knowing he could not rescind the invitation.

"No." Was the General's answer as the aliens marched up the ramp.

A communal sigh of relief filled the dome. Shaken, suddenly drained of energy, the Press Secretary plopped down in his seat. Images of scenarios involving the demon General perusing the streets played in his head and he shivered. The media pits were extremely quiet for what seemed like eternity. Cameramen slowly set their cameras down while reporters appeared to struggle with what to do next. Some slumped down in the seats, defeated as the onslaught of information sunk in. Then they sprung back to life. The next few decades were going to be busy news day.

TRUMP CARDS

Professor Bartley leaned on the edge of the viewing window, looking down on the activities occurring within the facility. From his vantage point he could see the observation rooms, medical wards and the cafeteria. Watching did not make him happy. He had stopped smiling long ago during his 'internship' at the previous facility. After two decades, his only priority was keeping his wards safe from society.

Now, there was the issue of needing soldiers for the coming war and the first thing the military requested were Bi-Genetics with talents. Since there was a good number of them accumulated over the years, they wanted a few trained in combat to hone their skills. He knew what they really wanted. Bioweapons: mass destructive power. Hand to hand combat was not part of their training agenda.

The commlink blinked on the console below him and he pressed it.

"What is it?"

"The testing area is ready. Who should we send first?" The male voice asked.

"Tommy. Then Janti. I want to know how powerful they can be."

"And then?" the male voice asked.

"We cut the data in half and record that." There was

silence from the commlink. "There is no reason for us to tell the military, or those disgusting scientists in charge, just how advanced we truly are."

"Agreed, sir." The commlink blinked off.

Professor Bartley let out a heavy sigh, hanging his head until his chin touched his chest. Looking back up, he caught his reflection on the glass. He had not physically aged a day since his twenty fifth birthday. Research concluded that Bi-Genetics aged slowly or only when they wanted. It made sense after seeing the aliens, who did not seem to age either. Slapping his hands down on the ledge, he pushed himself off and went to the other side of his domain to get a look at the testing area via monitors set up for his personal viewing.

Tommy was not happy either. He had been woken up from a dead sleep and dragged by force to a bunker where technicians held him down until further instructed. Just by scanning the room, noticing the control panels and shatter proof window, he knew it was a testing ground.

"Ow!" A technician had stuck a needle in his arm while he was distracted and injected a green liquid. "What the hell is that?" he demanded.

"Calorie booster to prevent you from passing out." The tech answered him.

"Or drop dead," the other smirked.

Tiny wireless electrodes were stuck to his forehead, chest and arms. The pneumatic door hissed open and he was dragged again out into the center of the test area. Tommy was getting angry. He could walk on his own two feet and didn't appreciate the brutality.

"Suck it up, kid," the first tech remarked.

"You're a telepath," Tommy stated.

"Good job. Now do a better one out here." The two techs left and when the doors shut behind them, the scenery changed into an open desert.

Soft, hot wind swirled around him and Tommy realized he really was in a desert. One of the techs must have been a teleporter. He looked around and saw no one else around. A click in his ear sounded and a voice came through.

"We want you to conjure up as much energy as you can and push it out. We will measure it from our end."

The voice was soothing.

"If you say so," Tommy replied, claiming defeat.

Taking a deep breath, he closed his eyes and focused all his telekinetic energy into a tight orb of light around him, holding it stable for a bit. If he was going to let it loose all wild like, he wanted to at least keep some level of control. The last thing he wanted was for anyone to know how much power he had, especially when even he didn't know himself. He opened his eyes and pushed a little. The orb expanded out about a thousand feet. He pushed a bit more and miscalculated. The orb went wide and traveled out of sight. Tommy felt like his body was being torn apart from the inside out. Icy needles of pain rushed through his veins and he screamed like he never had before. Right as he collapsed, emergency klaxons went off.

Inside the bunker located underground, the technicians watched in horror as the distance meter crept up to twelve miles before dissipating. The impact calculators on the barriers registered a shocking number. If the blast had been in an inhabited area, there would be nothing left in the area except human bodies with every bone broken from being crushed on contact.

"Get him back here and into the medical ward, stat!" The lead tester barked.

"Yes, sir!" The two technicians opened the door and teleported into the desert to retrieve Tommy who was a lump of unconscious dead weight.

"Professor?" The lead tester spoke into the monitor on the console.

"We tell no one."

"Agreed."

∽

General Hoskins scrolled through the data of candidates for his new Special Forces program made entirely of Bi-Genetics with talent. It took a word fight of epic proportion to convince those stuck up scientists to green light the project. They didn't want their precious specimens used as weapons.

Tough tits!

He snorted at his own inner remark. Those abominations were good for something. Many of the files contained teenagers between the ages of fifteen and seventeen and that's what he wanted; monsters in their prime.

One particular file caught his eye and he knew this one was Professor Makoto's pet assistant, Hana. He grinned, thinking of ways to get his clutches on the pretty little thing without incurring Professor Makoto's wrath. It could be done.

The automatic door slid open and his colleague, a Marine Admiral, strode in. A frown creased his brow and a fat file was tucked securely under one armpit. He stopped in front of Hoskins desk and slapped the folder onto its surface.

"The data from a testing ground at Facility Three." Hoskins slid it towards him. He opened it and flipped through the pages. It had been decided that hard copies were best in case they needed to be destroyed. This file was, in his opinion, useless.

"They're lying."

"Obviously. We know full well those kids are capable of much more output than this."

"We'll play their game, for now." Hoskins pushed the file back towards the Admiral. "I'll send a list of candidates shortly."

"Very well. I look forward to working with you, General."

"I, as well, General." He watched him leave and went back to his screen. Plans of mass Biode genocide played in his head.

"Tainted humans."

Darnizva sat lounging on the cushioned window seat in his living quarters while Zanzibar stood motionless staring out the viewing portal. Both were contemplating the best training method for the humans but so far, nothing came to mind that did not end in casualties. The human body was far more fragile than theirs and the only option would be to modify their DNA. He had heard some of the military leaders were recruiting Bi-Genetics for the front lines and it left a bad feeling in his abdomen. It smacked of ill-intentioned ulterior motive.

His chamber door slid open and Lieutenant Sspark entered without permission, as usual. He plopped down next to Darnizva and leaned back as if it were his own quarters.

"Oh, Darnizva! You're thinking too hard on this. If those humans are so willing to risk their lives for their planet, then let them."

"I do have offspring on Earth."

"And, I do not know why you did such a thing."

"No more so than you deciding to mate with my father." He glanced over at Sspark and saw his features scrunch up in defiance. "How does he fare these days?"

"If you went to him, you would know," Sspark spat. Not caring for his own lack of discipline when it came to that subject, he changed it back to the topic at hand. "Anyway, I am sure you will find a solution."

He slid further down on the cushioned counter, closing his eyes.

Zanzibar turned around at that moment and raised an eyebrow at Sspark, then Darnizva. All three of them were about the same age and the rife was palpable, stemming from Sspark's immaturity and arrogance. He was also the youngest. But make no mistake, they would kill for each other if facing an enemy. Darnizva watched Sspark fall deeper into sleep, then rose from his seat to join Zanzibar at the window.

"What do you think the human race's chances are against the Relliants, even with our assistance?" Zanzibar averted his gaze and crossed his arms. "That bad?" Zanzibar nodded. "An evacuation contingency?" Pursed lips were his reply. "Then, that's what we'll do when the time comes."

Outside the viewing portal, Earth loomed in front of them. The swirls of blue and white were mesmerizing. Darnizva felt pain knowing it would be forever changed in fifty years. He liked Earth.

⁓

The Russian Prime Minister sat across from the alien Amazonian Commander whose ship docked in their manufacturing town. A small entourage of Russian body guards were present in addition to hers. He felt small having to look up at her even when seated. A quick scan of the room and he saw the head of his military detail staring contently at her thighs. He didn't blame the man one bit. If it were not for the table between them, he would be doing the same.

"So, Mr. Prime Minister," she began.

"Yes, Commander Shatis Va?" He sat up straighter.

"How does your country train its warriors?"

Shatis Va picked up her fork and speared a piece of asparagus. She had voiced her opinion on how she found eating meat unpleasant but did enjoy the organic fare and starches. Taking a bite, she chewed and waited for his reply.

The Prime Minister thought for a moment.

"Well, we do a lot of weapons training and physical conditioning."

"No hand to hand combat?"

"Some, but it is used only if absolutely necessary. Say, like close encounter of the enemy."

"Hmm." Shatis Va sat back in her seat and also did some thinking. "So, your idea of war is to eliminate your targets from a distance to avoid interaction."

"We are not afraid of a fight," he balked.

"Then, why?"

"If we can save more lives in battle, then why tempt fate?"

"A valid point in light of your race. It would be in your best interest."

"What about our soon to be enemy?"

"Oh, they will no doubt come down to raze the surface personally. I believe your race does not have a weapon capable of firing long range into space to hit a target like one of their command ships."

She repositioned herself on the chair by crossing her legs the other way. The men in the room held their breath the short time it took for her to do so. Her white leotard never moved from where it should be yet they still hoped. As she took another bite of her steamed vegetables, the Prime Minister refocused on the conversation.

"If we were to have one, a weapon such as that, would we then have an advantage?"

"You would need more than one, my Prime Minister," she stated sweetly.

He visibly blushed, then cleared his throat when he saw his men stare at him in disbelief. For the hundredth time, he begged his wife's forgiveness.

"Of course, that would be ideal. Do you suppose we could have a tour of your ship soon? We have shown you our country and way of life."

"Possibly, but why? It's a battleship."

"That is correct."

Shatis Va pondered his reply for a moment and then exclaimed, "Oh!" She watched the smile on his face widen. "Of course!"

The Prime Minister knew Professor Pretchov would be glad to hear this once he reported back. They planned to develop something more advanced than what the Americans, helped by the alien they captured, were doing in reference to the new canon. A form of payback for being out of the data loop the past twenty odd years.

CHAPTER FOUR

KNOW THY ENEMY

That planet destroyer from a popular movie back in the twentieth century was Talley's first thought when he saw the massive ball of red and black moving slowly to the outskirts of Earth's orbit from behind. A swarm of tiny objects spewed out of it like insects forming an arc just within Earth space. He knew immediately that the enemy had arrived.

"I want constant visual on those ships and an ETA in case they decide to pay us a visit!" He commanded his crew. "Get the General on the line!"

"He's busy at the testing grounds for his project," his assistant replied.

"Shit, then get me someone with authority, dammit!"

"Yes sir."

From the monitors, the observation director gauged the design and color of the ships coming to the correct conclusion; they looked angry. He, too, felt a little hostile towards the Karysilans for crashing down on Earth and getting humans caught up in the middle of their war.

For the second time, the President of the United States was escorted to the domed arena for an audience with aliens. Though it might not go so well this time, he wondered what the enemy would be like and if he could negotiate with the help of the other world leaders.

Secretary of Defense, Eileen Regis kept herself close by. She was a former Marine and still practiced combat maneuvers in her spare time. If it came down to it, she would shove the secret service agents out of the way and get the job done herself, defending his life.

"Just so you know, Mr. President, we have the same exact audience as before. We felt there was no need to include anyone who wasn't privy the first time."

"Very good. Lord knows, we need to contain this thing even if the public has a little bit of knowledge." He saw the dignitaries and the media in their prospective areas looking more nervous than usual.

Ahead of him sitting on the other end of the field was the League's convoy ship with its ramp down and the officers already descending. Seeing General Phalkar gave him the shivers.

These are the good guys?

Shaking his head, the President went to his seat and noticed the large holoscreen floating in midair.

Silence enveloped the arena as the holoscreen flickered, a face appearing as it cleared. Pale skin, tar black hair and piercing blue eyes that seemed to glow stared back at them. His mouth, well-shaped yet thin, curved into a sinister smile as he laid eyes on the Karysilans.

"I see you have made yourselves at home on this planet," he began.

"He can speak English?" A General whispered to one of the President's cabinet members. "How?"

Looking up, he found those glowing blue eyes pierce him; rendering him speechless.

"We have warriors in your midst who report their interactions with your species on a regular basis. It was not that hard."

"Our kind has nothing to do with your war. There's

no need to involve us," the President piped in. He wanted to get negotiations rolling.

"Oh, but you see," the Relliant replied, "your planet has ample space to accommodate some of our race. I think we should occupy it."

"What…" the President's skin went pale. "…do you mean?"

"Our planet is overcrowded. We need a bigger one. Yours is ideal. If you will not comply," the leader lowered his head and his eyes slanted. "We will destroy it. And then, no one shall have it."

Darnizva clenched his fists tight and glanced back towards his father. They had talked with the President about this scenario possibly occurring but he had hoped not. General Phalkar's gaze did not waver from the Relliant leader's face. Mounting animosity electrified the arena.

The Relliant leader sat back from the monitor. Behind him was what appeared to be the main deck of a ship. Figures in dark uniforms moved around seeming oblivious to the conversation at hand. A closer look at the leader and it struck the President how young he appeared.

"But," he said, "I am not one to deny you a chance to defend yourselves. It wouldn't be any fun otherwise. Although the League has little faith in your ability to advance your technology tenfold in fifty years, I think it's sufficient."

"Wait a minute!" President demanded. "What about your spies on our planet?"

"Oh. They will not act until it is time." He smiled then and added another shocking fact. "By the way, a few other species from our galaxy snuck in and bred with your kind." His gaze turned to General Phalkar. "Once a pathway is established, any species capable of travelling them would be curious to see where it goes."

"Who?" Admiral Goulld spoke for the first time, his voice boomed even though he spoke softly. Many in the audience cringe. His golden colored eyes burned.

"Hmm," the Relliant leader tilted his head to the side and looked up into the air. "Possibly a Senigranke or two, and maybe a few of those flower species."

"Did you just say Senigrankes?" Ammordia whispered.

"I'd wish you good luck, but I will not be denied."

With that, the transmission ended.

Deep silence hit the dome once more and President Pulham stared down at the Karysilans who looked a little more than upset. A pained expression crossed Darnizva's face and it triggered panic in him.

"What are Senigrankes, Captain Darnizva?" All eyes shifted to the Captain.

"How shall I put this?" He rubbed his jaw for a bit then dropped his arms down to his sides. "They are a race of carnivores. Of course, some have evolved to the point of knowing how to hunt discreetly."

"When you say carnivores…."

"I mean they eat other species for food."

Even the darkest of skin lost some color as those in attendance concluded what that meant. Serial killers on the loose was one thing, but alien man eaters were not something they knew how to deal with.

"And these flower people?" the President dreaded even asking. "They sound harmless enough."

"Yes, they can be, unless provoked."

"And then?"

"They can annihilate an entire planet in an instant."

"You're joking?" General Hoskins was getting more disgusted by the minute.

"The flower species known as Dassranians, are a

hybrid race, half Creator and half Destroyer, who create these amazing life forces resembling flowers that breathe to replenish a planet's atmosphere. But, they also have the power to wipe out every living thing so it was deemed best to keep them away from other species. Thus, they were sent to flourish on a world of their own."

"Can we find these creatures and contain them? These Seni whatever's and flower people?" General Hoskins demanded.

Fuck if it ain't one thing and not the other! He cursed to himself.

"I doubt that. If they have not been clearly seen, then they must have learned to adapt to the environment here on Earth."

"So, now what?" The Prime Minister of Russia asked, directing his question to the scientists.

They were all discussing something in low voices amongst themselves so no one else could hear.

Professor Pretchov leaned forward.

"I believe it is imperative that we not only raise the timeline of our recruitment but get every weapons specialist on board to create new ones capable of proving that monster wrong."

"But first," Professor Makoto interjected, "A press conference. We should alert the world now that it has come to this. Put the rumor mills to rest." He turned to the Karysilans. "Agreed?"

The aliens responded with nods. In addition, Sspark snorted in disgust. The League officers turned and headed back into the convoy. They surely had a plan of their own to devise.

CHILDREN OF WAR

Janti tapped his study booklet on the desk in a steady rhythm while he stared out into nothingness. He had long tuned out the scenery before him and relished the calm. Class was over but many of the students stayed to socialize until the next bell. He was bored as usual with the curriculum, his I.Q. off the charts even for an advanced human. What went through his mind now was the sorry excuse for a press conference everyone had to watch regarding the impending alien war.

Out of the corner of his eye he saw Tommy walk down the hallway to class located in a room across the way. Tommy may not be as smart as him, but he was just as powerful because Janti could feel it oozing off him. His own testing was coming along nicely since, unlike Tommy, he had no qualms about letting everyone know how much energy he could push out.

He had met a few other Bi-Genetics who were not part of the facility but held captive by their government for 'observation'. A frown creased his brow thinking about the way they were treated. It was worse than animals. Being tested along with other children in the facility for the sole purpose of finding bioweapons was no surprise. One thing was certain; General Hoskins was a hateful prick and Professor Lancaster was not to be trusted, making him overly protective of Tommy.

"Hey, Janti!"

A classmate called from across the room.

"Yeah?" He blinked, focusing on his surroundings.

"They say Professor Lancaster is coming for another visit. He's going to give us a pep talk on what the war means for," he put up his fingers and made quotation marks in the air, "all of us."

"Right," Janti grunted.

"Are you going?"

"What?"

"To the auditorium to hear what he has to say?"

"Hell no!"

"Well," the classmate shrugged. "Suit yourself. Class is cancelled for the rest of the day because of it. See ya."

As the class headed out for the event, Janti stood and decided to grab Tommy when he came out of his classroom. It was time for a serious talk. No more stupid destructive arguments they both regretted afterwards. They were soul mates and could not be without each other no matter how they felt. Not knowing the outcome of humans, he was not going to waste any more time.

⌒

Willing to comply, albeit furious, Professor Makoto watched as the electrodes were attached to Hana's flawless skin. The poor thing looked nervous and scared but put on a brave face for him when they made eye contact. General Takayama stood next to him outside the viewing room with a gleam in his eyes Professor Makoto did not like. He felt his authority was being slowly taken away as the years progressed with more stressing issues coming to light.

"I'm sure you understand, we have to assess every Bi-Genetic with even the remote of talents to cover our bases," the General stated.

MAQUEL A. JACOB

"Of course," the Professor replied, not severing his gaze from Hana who smiled softly at him. "We must do what is best for humanity."

"I'm glad you concur." The General tapped on the glass and the lead tester nodded.

The technician stood in front of Hana, blocking his view to check the electrodes and make sure the data registered on the equipment. Satisfied, he stepped back and went to his terminal inside a separate tempered glass bunker. An initial analysis of Hana's talents assured him it was a satisfactory precautionary measure. The young man was not powerful enough to destroy the base.

"Okay, Hana," he began. "I want you to focus all of your energy into a ball that surrounds you. When you feel like it is stable enough, you are going to expand the bubble as far as you can, as quickly as you can, without losing control."

"Okay." Hana replied in his small voice.

Professor Makoto felt his chest tighten and when he turned to the General, his stomach lurched at the man's eager eyes drinking in the scene. He waited for the military man to start licking his lips and didn't have to wait long to witness it.

The bubble of energy became visible almost instantly and apparent that Hana was unable to keep a grasp on it. Sweat poured out of every inch of his body and his eyes flashed bright. A shockwave hit the walls, shaking the building and cracking the tempered glass barrier. Blood spewed out of Hana's mouth and his body slumped in the harness.

"No!" Professor Makoto shouted. "No, no, no!" He pounded the glass in desperation.

"Relax, Professor" General Takayama purred. "Those things can heal at a fast rate. He just broke most of the bones in his body. He should be good as new in a few weeks, yes?" Professor Makoto stared at him in horror. "Of course, now we know he is not viable. You can have your pet back."

"Hana is not a pet or a THING!" Professor Makoto snapped. "They are human, just like us!"

"No, they are not." The General turned to leave.

"Yes, that's right. They are more evolved than us Regular humans. Advanced humans make us feel obsolete, yes?"

The General didn't turn around but stopped his stride.

"There is no need for humans to advance in this stage of evolution."

When General Takayama entered the elevator and the doors closed, Professor Makoto pushed the sensor that opened the bay doors.

"You're wrong, General. We need to advance now more than ever."

He went into the testing area to assist with retrieving Hana. If the World Military was going to play games and insist on super soldiers, he had an even more sinister resolution in mind. It was all about timing.

With the thought of impending doom circulating throughout the masses, new battles raged on Earth pitting human against human in a fight for territory. A recent census found that many people felt they could weather the war by being in certain underground areas. Prime sectors were marked and a fire fight unleashed.

This all played right into General Hoskins' hands, giving him an excuse to test out his new soldiers in rebel territories. Internal mini cameras had been injected into their eyes so he, and his personnel, could watch their actions in real time. He wished it was something he had thought of first but good old Professor Lancaster had come up with the idea.

"Bring up Terror Eight," he instructed the technician below.

He named them Terrors instead of agents or giving them military rankings because they were anomalies, tools to be used and discarded.

"Make sure our troops are evacuated from the area before it's sent down."

"Yes, sir!"

Terror Eight was fifteen. His hatred for the military was justified and he knew it would not be this way forever. Doing what he was told bought his people time. They could all easily wipe out everyone and everything but it would defeat the purpose of being accepted as normal human beings. And, yes, he was a terror by definition. His ability included razing an entire five-mile radius to dust, sparing nothing.

"Terror Eight!" The earbud commlink squawked. "Confirm drop point and commence operation. Target area is two kilometers. Maintain distance from friendlies."

"Roger that, Command."

His dark hair flew back as he opened the side door of the helicopter. Leaning over he saw the target below and glanced over to the right to see how far away the cavalry had gotten after fleeing the scene. The rebels looked triumphant.

He leapt out of the helicopter and made a straight dive for the middle of the town. About five hundred feet before hitting the ground, he formed an energy bubble around him and flipped upright, landing on his feet. He spread his arms wide and smiled at the rebels who seemed perplexed by his arrival, unsure whether to fire their weapons.

That's when the shockwave hit them as the bubble surrounding Terror Eight expanded, engulfing everything, disintegrating all. The entire area resembled a desert shaped in a perfect circle. Dust swirled around in the aftermath, finally settling along the edges. Above, the helicopter returned for his hasty retrieval. Quick and dirty. He nodded to himself in satisfaction as he climbed up the rope ladder that dropped down and rode suspended in midair for a while before going in.

〜

Professor Morandi found herself in front of a mirror admiring her features until she caught the sly smile on her face. Since assimilating alien DNA into her system nearly forty years ago, the aging process had slowed to a crawl, almost halting. She had watched her male colleagues revel in it by ditching their wives and chasing after younger female fare. They were all pushing the eighty mark, some already past it, and no intentions of letting themselves go before saving the planet or at the very least, resolve the discrimination issues for Bi-Genetics.

The whole super soldier program was a travesty her colleagues and she had tried to prevent with Professor Lancaster as the exception, authorizing it behind their backs. She resented his assumption that it was necessary and that they were equally on board. A file she had previously ruffled through lay on her desk. Bi-Genetics with talent were one in a thousand or more. Rare, but with the world population churning out nearly 20% of its number as advanced humans, there were more than the military could have hoped for.

She squeezed the bridge of her nose with her thumb and forefinger, taking a deep breath.

Tapping the intercom button, she summoned her assistant.

"Kevin!"

"Yes, Ma'am?" A silky tenor male voice replied through the speaker.

"Get in here!"

"Of course, Ma'am."

The office door swung open and a tall, sandy brown-haired man in a grey suit stood in the doorway. His piercing grey eyes were partially covered by long strands of hair hanging haphazardly forward.

Gods, he's beautiful! She couldn't help thinking to herself.

It took all the strength she had not to go over, push his hair back and caress his face. She had never touched him nor planned to.

"I told you to not call me Ma'am!"

"My apologies…" he stopped before calling her that again, seeing the look of warning.

"I want you to take a look at this." She pointed to the file, not wanting to touch it again.

He strode across the room in three steps due to his height and with one finger flipped it open. It rose off the desk and positioned in front of him, the pages turning rapidly to the end before it dropped into his outstretched hand.

"Interesting."

"They will come for you too, I'm sure of it."

"Are you worried about me?"

His tone was condescending and she showed her distaste by frowning. He smiled.

"This is serious!" She snapped.

"Let them come. I am not so weak that I'd die from something like this." She felt her skin go pale with fear and saw the regret on his face the moment he finished saying it. Reaching over, his fingers brushed against her cheek to wipe away a lonely tear running down it. "If you want me to defend myself, I will."

"I won't let them take you again. What they did to you was monstrous." She leaned on the desk supporting her weight with her arms.

"This?" He wagged the file.

"I don't want to see that again, either."

"A copy?"

"Of course. They wouldn't dare give us the real thing." A flash of orange made her glance up and she saw the file go up in a fiery blaze until there was nothing left. "That's not what I meant. We could have used some of the data."

"For what, exactly?"

'I don't know! Something!" Exasperated she went around and plopped into her chair.

Kevin studied her for a moment, and she remembered the first time they met twenty years ago during a raid of the experiment camp he was enslaved in. Seeing the look of horror on her face when she burst into the makeshift lab and half the children dead, the rest on their way made up his mind if she was friend or foe. The new super soldier programs forced down the scientists' throats by the military did not sit well with him either.

"They're coming." He said to her telepathically.

Her head snapped up higher.

"How long?" She asked.

He hit the Allcom and gave a command.

"Do not let one soldier enter this facility. Use force if necessary, but no casualties unless they decide to provoke the issue." He looked up at Professor Morandi. "What do you want to do with the leader?"

"What?" She was confused.

"Captivity, torture?"

"We're capturing an entire retrieval team?" She exclaimed, incredulous.

"Why, of course. Give them a taste of their own medicine, if you will."

"If you insist." She let out a sigh. "I just don't want to know about it."

"Agreed."

Kevin turned to the door and whipped off his suit jacket, tossing it on the table by the door. He rolled up his sleeves as he went into the hall.

"I'm off. Cheer for me?"

"Buona caccia," She waved him off.

The Army General was not happy with the stalled progress of getting into the Italian facility to retrieve the prized specimens for his new super soldier unit. It would be his third and the candidates in the building ahead were exceptional, in his opinion. Especially the Professor's pet assistant. He knew where the boy had come from and felt he was merely returning stolen military property.

Meeting resistance was not part of the plan. None of the other Professors whose facilities he had raided made a stink so why this one? That uppity bitch. He wondered how much power she thought she had these days to defy the military. One if his men came running towards him interrupting his thoughts.

"Sir, we can't seem to get a clear path to either of the entrances. We may have to find another way in."

"Then, that's what we'll do. Get a blueprint of the layout."

"Sir?"

"That's what hackers are for, soldier!" He snapped. "Get to it!"

"Yes sir!"

The soldier ran off to the technology van positioned in the formation's rear.

"This will teach you to fuck with me, you old cunt," The General spat.

Just as planned.

Kevin smirked as he watched the General and his soldiers break through two emergency bunker entries. He knew they weren't going to give up, deciding to find an alternate way in. It was also obvious that the General would want to come and give the Professor a hard time himself. Pinpointing the General's exact location, he went to personally crack a few bones as a greeting and teach him a lesson instead.

"Here I come, General."

The corridors filled with gun smoke from the semiautomatic rifles rapid fire in a closed space. Every round fell short of their target as four office workers stood side by side across the threshold forming an invisible barricade, stopping them halfway. It went on for about two minutes until the soldiers retreated down the hall and threw a grenade. The barricade tightened around the four and shielded them from the blast.

Scorch marks covered the walls and floor but there was no other damage. The facility was built to sustain a nuclear blast. As the first wave of soldiers re-entered the corridor, the smoke barely cleared, two of the workers shot forward in faster than light sprints to engage the enemy while the other two remained blocking further infiltration of the building.

At the main cargo hold on the same side as the office suites, Kevin waited patiently along with three of his own personal assistants for the General. They stood behind him in silent anticipation. It wasn't every day their got to use their talents. He could hear the gunfight going on just outside and shook his head, disappointed with the General's decision to use force.

The cargo doors were forced open and a group of ten soldiers spilled in with the General and two guards following behind. They slowed their advance and eased up about two hundred feet from Kevin before halting, guns raised, red laser sights making a straight-lined grid.

"Well, well," the General started. "How generous of you to come on your own. I didn't have to chase you after all." Kevin and his entourage did not move. "Just in case you think this will be easy, I must warn you we have developed a nice little restraint module to prevent you from using those nasty talents of yours."

His eyes gleamed.

"Oh, I know," Kevin replied.

His hand swiped across the room, the first row of soldiers lifting into the air and following its trajectory into the far wall. They dropped in a pile. Rounds from the second row's rifles slowed to a stop inches before the three men and before they could hit the ground, useless, they were reversed and sent back, taking down the five soldiers.

"Stop them!" The General screamed at his two guards as he watched them pushing the buttons on the modules. "What are you waiting for?" He turned back to the fighting and found himself staring into the cold grey eyes of Kevin. A loud cracking sound filled his ears and blood bubbled up his esophagus then out of his mouth.

"Mmm, that must have hurt." Kevin cooed. "Don't worry, it's just a few ribs puncturing some tissue, possibly an organ." He slapped the modules out of the two guards' hands then backhanded them to the ground in one swing. "You shouldn't play with dangerous toys."

"The other team reports capture of the other soldiers.

Where do you want these?" The nearest assistant inquired.

"Put them in the lower cells on the east wing."

"And the General?"

Kevin made eye contact with the General who still looked defiant. He set him gently on the floor of the cargo hold and walked away.

"Make sure he gets medical attention then put him in the testing lab." The General's eyes went wide. "Professor Morandi has given me authorization to do as I please with you and your men. Isn't that sweet of her?" He left the hold and went to the elevator previously left open for him. Today was going to be a fun day.

MAQUEL A. JACOB

RELLIANT INCOGNITOS

Velvet curtains parted revealing the spacious stage where a single man in a matador's costume stood in the center spotlight. The orchestra below made ready to start on queue as the audience held its breath. The most renown opera singer in the country was about to cast his spell on them and it was exactly what they paid for.

Standing six feet eight inches tall with pale skin and jet-black hair slicked back into a tight ponytail that lay down his back, Geoffrey Hagen commanded unwavering attention with striking blue eyes the color of electricity. He made no excuses for his decisions or personality and just did his job better than the rest. This is what separated him from all the other male opera singers in the industry.

Watching the audience sit mesmerized by his voice as he sang an aria in perfect Italian with a flawless alto, hitting a soprano note and holding it when the piece called for it, he wondered what it would have been like if he had been born on this planet.

Such simple creatures, he mused while moving into the finale of the song. As he finished, there was hushed silence, then an uproar of applause. Bowing in response, he left the stage and waited for his cue to return for the standing ovation and rose tossing.

"Ah!" His manager came bustling in the dressing room unannounced. "My dear Geoffrey, you were
174

amazing, as always!" He gushed.

"Get out of my dressing room before I snap you in half."

"Let's not get so violent," the man laughed nervously.

"What do you want?" Geoffrey found that in the entertainment industry, threats of violence were not taken seriously. It was like a term of endearment. Thus, he gave up on following through with his threats. More bees with honey.

"The strangest thing, really." His manager settled himself on a folding chair in the corner. "A very popular rock group sent over tickets to their show. They seem to be great fans of yours. The show is next week."

"That's not unusual. Have you forgotten I used to be in a very successful Rock band before coming back to doing full opera again?"

"Oh!" his manager pulled on his lower lip. "I had forgotten. Not my genre of music, really. Oh, well!" He slapped his thigh. "Shall I RSVP?"

"Sure, do as you like."

Geoffrey waited until his manager left the room to let out a long sigh as he slumped backwards in the chair and let his head hang. His undone hair spilled over the back in shiny black tendrils while his arms hung limp on the sides. Sometimes, the shows were exhausting and he missed the old days. Touring on a huge bus, being surrounded by giant speakers that shook an entire stadium and groupies (the young kind unlike in opera), were some of the best things he had experienced. Earth's concept of music and the business surrounding it fascinated him.

It sounded nostalgic to his ears and he decided to make a night of it. Just the anticipation of feeling the floor vibrate from the reverb of a bass guitar sent chills up his spine. Sitting upright, he peeked at himself in the mirror. Not bad for what in Earth years was eighty- five.

He didn't look a day past forty and his real age was much more than that.

"A heavy metal band, huh?"

᠊᠊᠊

Rock politics.

Geoffrey almost vocally spat out as he was ushered through the VIP area by four bouncers who could pass for escaped convicts. His manager thought fans of a heavy metal group would recognize a famous opera singer and need additional protection. Because of all the hoops his people had to jump through just to get in, he had missed the preshow Meet and Greet. Now, he was being rushed to his seat to watch the band who invited him, Fisting Pamela, do their thing.

He vaguely remembered them from the early days as a Goth Rock group in the nineties. It was a horrible name for a band and he couldn't figure out for the life of him how they kept female fans. He had not heard any of their new music yet but had a hunch it was just as politically incorrect as before in every way; especially towards women.

A sense of relief and excitement came over him when he noticed his seat was high above near the bigger than life wall of speakers situated on either side of the stage. Looking down into the floor section reminded him of the insane mosh pits he witnessed during his performances as a Rock God. The audience was already primed with angst and sweat by the opening band who just finished not fifteen minutes ago. As much as he would love to get in there, his manager would have a coronary.

"Would you like a beverage, Mr. Hagen?" A man in a suit tapped his shoulder.

"A...what?" Geoffrey let out a small laugh. This man was clearly a corporate music executive's flunky out on a mercy errand for the band. "Just get me a beer, man."

Embarrassed, the man nodded and backed away from him. The roadies nearby laughed at him, one even slapping his back as he passed. He disappeared into the room below and a few minutes later came back with two bottles of domestic. Glass was only allowed in the VIP section. Everyone else had to consume their alcohol in clear plastic cups from the vendor stations. Geoffrey thanked him and cracked open the first beer he had in months.

Flashes of lights and the smoke machine cranking prevented Geoffrey from seeing the band clearly but he was right about the music. Some of the lyrics even he found offensive and that was hard to do considering his past debauchery on the road. The crowd ate it up and women screamed while flashing their breasts for all to see. He saw them go wild with lust as the lead singer took a swig of whiskey straight from the bottle and spewed onto the exposed breasts in the front row.

He sat in shock as the crowd pounded the floor for an encore and Fisting Pamela obliged with two more songs of equally disgusting material. Eight beers had not made his mind foggy enough not to care about that, solidifying his conclusion that Rock and Roll had evolved for the worst.

Back stage, he waited along with other celebrity fans for his turn to meet the band. Requested to go last, he found it strange when everyone except the band were ushered out of the room. Their manager gave the green light for him to enter and when he did, he understood the reason for his invitation.

"Holy Shit, man!"

The lead singer stumbled forward, hand out-stretched. As he clasped Geoffrey's hand, making a loud clack, he used his other arm to wipe his nose with the sleeve of his shirt.

"Fuck, dude! You're like a rock legend and shit, now!"

Geoffrey checked out the man's bleached out hair sticking out in all directions and the quasi goth look, complete with a blood red velvet vest. His stage attire had not changed over the years. The mascara had long lost its battle with the heated gel lights, making his face more of a ghoul's than a vampire's. He glanced over at the other three members of the band and found the drummer having no interest in meeting him whatsoever. Arrogance oozed from him. Back to the lead singer, he forced his hand out of the man's grip during a full shake to make it seem natural.

What a disgusting creature.

The bass player was tall, skinny and pale with black hair down to his waist. The guitar player was similar, except with a lot more muscle and darker skin tone. Both had blue eyes that glinted like jewels in the light. They both stood up and made their way over to greet him.

"How you doing?"

The guitar player's grip was firm and steady, his voice not quite a baritone. His thick black hair swung with every movement. They made direct eye contact.

The bass player came up and shook his hand next. His hair was bone straight even after being whipped around on stage under the stage lights.

"Hello, sir. Great to me you," he said softly.

The lead singer was still beaming and rubbing his fingers in his scalp, admiring the fact that he was in the same room as an icon. Movement from the couch made them all turn to see the drummer lean forward and raise two fingers. He waved them twice.

"Yeah, real honor." With that he sat back and stretch his legs out.

Geoffrey just stared at him for a moment.

Fuck head.

The drummer left a bad taste in his mouth and he wanted to hurt him; badly. He turned his attention to the lead singer who saw it as his invitation to speak.

"Oh man, I was kinda' shocked when Craig and Bree here," he motioned to the guitar player then the bassist, "suggested we invite you since your show was around the same time as ours."

"Is that right?"

"Aww, you should have came on stage and sung with us!"

The thought made Geoffrey cringe. No way in hell would he be caught dead or otherwise on stage with those heathens, the drummer and vocalist respectively. He felt sorry for Craig and Bree. As much as he loved the concept of music, there were some who didn't quite understand its intrigue and fucked it up royally. Fisting Pamela was living proof.

"Yes, well, logistics had me running late so I barely got to my seat to see the show."

"Fucking bureaucrats, man. It's all politics in this industry." He pulled out his phone to check it and slapped himself in the forehead. "I gotta' get going! They want me to do this thing without the rest of the guys." Slapping his hand into Geoffrey's, he said, "It was so awesome to meet you! You gotta' come check us out again!"

Seeing the vocalist leave, the drummer got up and stood to his full height of six feet seven inches. It took three steps for him to get to the door and as he crossed paths with Geoffrey, stated, "I'm out." Leaving just the Craig and Bree.

"Lieutenants."

"Commander." They replied in unison.

Without wasting a moment, he stepped towards them.

"Where, in the living fuck, did you find those two?" He asked bluntly.

Bree's soft facial features scrunched up, clearly upset by the question. Craig fell into the bean bag chair against the wall and let out a bored sigh. Bree's focus snapped back to Geoffrey.

"They were a means to an end. In this business, sometimes a few raunchy band members are a good thing."

"Did you watch our General's childish display of power?"

"He's still quite young." Craig sat up to get more comfortable. "He will never be a great General like his father."

"Very true. But, he is our leader so we must adhere to his agenda."

"Do we?"

One of Craig's eyebrows shot up as he asked.

"Careful, soldier," Geoffrey chided. "I control the Command Fleet."

"Yet, you would never turn us in for insubordination."

Bree slid onto the counter, his head hung low. There was silence as Geoffrey and Craig watched him contemplating. Finally raising his head, he stared deep into Geoffrey's eyes.

"What if we don't want to destroy Earth?"

"I figured you would say something like that," Geoffrey replied. "I feel the same. But, until we can come up with a solution, the plan for takeover or destruction is in play." Bree nodded in defeat. "And, for all that is mighty, find a new venture. Or, better yet, go solo."

Craig let out a chuckle and eased himself out of plushy seat. "But, that would not be any fun. Come on, how could you not find those two entertaining?"

"I'd rather take a razor blade shower than spend another two minutes with them."

This time, Craig laughed out loud.

"Let's go get some real drinks."

At six feet five inches tall, he was intimidating to most, but not to his commanding officer. He curled a finger at Bree who slipped off the counter to stand at equal height and join them.

Outside, their manager was talking on the phone so didn't notice the three slip away, avoiding all the body guards and media. Geoffrey knew the poor bastard was going to have hell to pay when the company found out. For now, he was glad to hang out with his officers after decades of being incognito.

The bar was a musician's mecca, packed mostly with rock stars and up comers chilling out between tour dates or on hiatus. Run by an old former bouncer, the place had everything a rocker on the lam needed; pool tables, dart boards, air hockey and plenty of booze. Mostly booze. Long bars with soft amber lighting ran along the walls while the main bar, lit up with green lights, took up the rear back wall. Round tables were scattered in the center and square ones sat along the edges where the noise wasn't as loud. Big screens hung from the ceiling at strategic areas of the room for easy viewing.

"Another night of mayhem, I see."

Geoffrey smiled at the sight of drunk musicians getting belligerent with each other over nothing. He glanced back at Craig and Bree who just stood in the doorway looking exhausted.

Understandable after having to work so hard with a shitty band for nearly two hours.

"Pull yourselves together and have a few drinks with me before you crash."

"We have about two hours before our manager goes ape shit and comes looking for us," Craig said.

Bree blinked at that revelation and slumped further. Geoffrey realized they were not in any shape to fight if it came down to it. Being on Earth had made them soft, he thought. Craig staggered past him and went to the nearest long bar.

Sitting down, Geoffrey tapped the barman hurrying pass and ordered a bottle of tequila. He didn't have to say what kind because everything in the bar was top shelf. No street juice here, only the best. When the bottle came with three shot glasses, he poured and distributed them.

"To victory," he announced softly as he raised his glass, chucking the burning liquid down his throat.

"Yeah, victory," Craig replied doing the same.

"Victory," Bree whispered. His face crinkled as the tequila hit his throat.

"So," Geoffrey slammed his shot glass on the bar. "I have a training sector set up. I think you should brush up on your skills."

"It's that obvious, isn't it?" Craig poured himself and Bree another shot.

"As your commanding officer, it is my duty to make sure you are ready for battle."

"We will be." Craig took his shot and held the tiny glass to his forehead.

"There are four more shows and then we can start training," Bree added.

He took his shot and this time managed to get it down easy.

"Good, I look forward to seeing your progress."

A gust of wind swept through the bar as the doors were thrown open. Wild eyed, his suit disheveled under a long tan trench coat, stood Fisting Pamela's manager gripping his phone like a vise.

"God damnit!" He marched towards the long bar where the three of them were sitting and halted a few feet from Craig. "What the hell do you think this is? A game?" His voice rose with every syllable. "Don't you EVER do something like this again!" Turning away from them and heading for the door, he commanded, "Get up! The limo is waiting to take you back to the hotel. You have a flight tomorrow." Realization struck and he turned back around wide eyed again. "Oh, God! Mr. Hagen, I am so sorry. You wanted to have some alone time with them, didn't you?"

"That's correct." Geoffrey was not amused with the man's outburst.

"You see…"

"Yes, they have a flight in the morning to their next gig. I understand that better than anyone."

His gaze burned into the manager's.

"I am so sorry. I can have the limo wait as long as you like. Your PR guy was not worried about you in the least. Now I know why."

"Would you like to stay a little longer?" He asked Craig and Bree.

Craig looked over at Bree and saw him asleep sitting up with the shot glass still in his hand. He himself didn't look too alert. Pouring one more shot, he downed it and shook his head.

"I think we're toast, sir."

"Very well." Geoffrey stood up, towering over the manager. "If you would please escort us to our ride."

In the limousine Geoffrey made a note of the sorry state his officers were in. If his top two soldiers were out of shape, he couldn't imagine what the others were like. At least he had a good twenty-five to thirty years to get them back in gear.

CHAPTER FIVE

TESTING THE WATERS

Too much light.

Grannalt thought as he was ushered, hands bound so he couldn't shield his eyes from the assault from the lab's giant bay windows. After nearly forty years on Earth, his captives still did not trust him which was asinine because one, they needed him, and two, his commander knew he was here. He imagined if a whiff of what they had really been doing do him all this time came to light, a river of blood would flow through the bunker.

On the far right of the lab sat the bottom platform of the skyscraper sized canon built over the last ten years to give Earth a foothold in alien combat. It tilted forward aiming at the heavens. The two orderlies placed him at the base where its control room was located and the restraints were removed.

"My sincere apologies, Grannalt." The senior advisor made his way towards him, a crooked smile crept on his face. "It has come to pass that we are quite ashamed of our treatment towards you all these decades. Rest assured, there will be no more of," he waved a hand in the air, "this, of course. We would like very much if you would continue to help us, despite that."

Grannalt stared at him while his body drained of energy and emotion. He had been poked, prodded, cut open, raped and impregnated many times over losing all hope. Even when the ships came to the surface, his captors refused to let him go. Their experiments and torture continued though lessened to a degree. Now, they wanted him to dismiss it all and become one of their scientific soldiers?

"I can understand your misgivings. But, your race is willing to assist us and as a soldier, you should follow the example of your superior officers."

"Why won't you kill me?" Grannalt whispered as his head hung down to his chest. The dingy hospital robe, his only wardrobe, slipped to one shoulder.

The senior advisor reached over and pulled the fabric back up. He knelt beside Grannalt. A look of pity and remorse replacing the crooked smile.

"One thing I do know is that Professor Lancaster would have never let you die. In his own twisted way, he was fascinated with you. Now that he's gone into hiding, his son has taken over and has no use for you in his studies. But, we need you to put the finishing touches on the canon."

"Let me go." Grannalt pleaded softly.

"I can't do that." The senior advisor shook his head. "I can make your life better here, though. I promise, after you are done with the firing test, I'll get you settled."

Grannalt looked up at the inner hull of the cannon's base, tears rolling down his cheeks. He had never shed so much fluid from his eyes until he came to Earth. He now knew what true sorrow and pain was.

"Why?" He asked turning to the senior advisor.

"Until this war is over and Captain Darnizva comes for you, we are to keep you safe."

His eyes widened in disbelief. There was no guarantee that any of them, human or alien, would survive the battle against the Relliants. It was all just wishful thinking. Realizing he may never see his home or family again, let alone his own battalion, he wiped his face with the back of his forearm and nodded.

"Good. I'm glad."

The senior advisor let out a slow breath.

Standing up, he went to the middle of the lab and pressed the Allcom button on the raised console. He cleared his throat for effect and began his spiel.

"Ladies, gentlemen! As you know, it has been a long time in the making, but we have a functioning cannon capable of hitting targets in space. This was no small feat and with the help of our resident Karysilan, Grannalt, we have achieved a milestone in weapons technology. In twenty minutes, we will be firing a test round for a target sent previously into orbit. Let's get started!"

His declaration sent everyone scrambling to tasks.

A glance at Grannalt made him take hold of the nearest scientist walking by.

"I need you to get him some clothes, a bath, everything and anything to keep him comfortable to deter from killing himself. Do you understand how important he is?"

"Of course! We all do," the scientist snapped. "I'll get him what he needs."

"Thank you." He let them go back to their tasks.

It had taken almost three years to convince Professor Lancaster that Grannalt was no longer feasible and another six months with his arrogant son to feel the same before the alien was turned over to him. Unlike many of the higher ups, he did not see the aliens as threats deserving of abuse. He endured witnessing the sick treatment of Grannalt until there was a decent plan to set him free. Looking at the young alien, he felt ashamed as a human being.

We don't treat animals this awful.

Warning sirens wailed as the larger than life digital

counter lit up to start the countdown. Airspace had been cleared for miles beyond the projected radius of the blast because the numbers were speculative.

"Tee minus twelve minutes." The lab's female AI announced.

"Places people!"

Grannalt worked the controls and started the sequence that powered up the core five hundred feet directly above him. It was a newly created mineral the size of a boulder held suspended by magnetic polarity inside the launch chamber. Tiny tendrils of electricity danced around it, causing a strange humming he could feel through his whole body. He was scared.

"Initiating firing sequence. Opening chamber." The loud whirring of the cannon's eye waking up was like nails on a chalk board. "Positioning cannon." It shifted down ten degrees then to the left, locking in place with a loud boom. "Tee minus thirty seconds."

Everyone took deep breaths and adjusted their ear protectors. The counter seemed to speed up while the AI counted down from ten. The senior advisor turned to see Grannalt not wearing any protective gear. Too late.

Grannalt fired the cannon and his entire body revolted from the shockwave. He involuntarily vomited, blood pouring out of his ears as he lost consciousness and slid to the floor convulsing. His thoughts echoed into the senior advisor's mind.

I'm dying. I'm finally dying.

Forgoing the awesome sight of the giant beam of energy tearing through the air, four of the scientists followed the senior advisor as he raced to Grannalt's side. Even with the ear protection, the sound of the cannon fire still rang in their heads.

Hairline fractures formed on the bay windows but they somehow remained intact. Grannalt was held down and a twisted-up piece of his gown was shoved in his mouth to prevent him from swallowing his own tongue. They were not going to lose him now. Not after all of this.

General Hoskins watched with anticipation, as did all the other personnel in the observation room, at the cannon's beam, measuring a quarter mile in width, scorch the air towards its target in space. He was mesmerized by its sheer power, the damn thing causing a mini earthquake when it fired. All it needed to do now was obliterate its target and they were home free.

"Liking our new toy, I see."

General Perrara waltzed onto the observation deck looking pristine as usual. Hoskins despised the man.

"Oh, we have to wait and see, but I think we have a winner even if it doesn't perform."

"Oh?" Perrara's forehead raised.

"We can always tweak the damn thing."

"Good point. So?" He nodded towards the viewing monitor.

"We'll know in about two minutes." Hoskins felt his cheesy grin deepen. "Those damn aliens are good for something."

General Perrara frowned.

"You do understand that they are far more advanced than we are and could easily take over?"

"The hell you say?" Hoskins whirled on him. "No aliens are going to come and take us down! We're fucking Americans!"

"Yes, that's all well and good, but this is not some science fiction movie where we get to win because we have some baseless faith in humanity."

Hoskins, shaking with fury stepped towards Perrara but didn't get far as the whole room went into an uproar. He turned to the vidscreen and saw the target breaking apart into smithereens. Sounds of disappointment, mixed with joy, were heard around the room.

"I guess you're going to have to tweak the damn thing after all. Your target wasn't turned to vapor. See you at the next test, General." Perrara swaggered out of the room, leaving Hoskins in a state of confusion.

"There wasn't sufficient output to vaporize the target," the chief engineer began to explain. "As awesome as it seemed, it basically only knocked on the surface."

"I don't think this facility can handle anything more powerful. That blast caused a category two earthquake. It wasn't much but it sure shook the shit out of everything. Not to mention the shatter proof observation windows," one of his colleagues added.

"I understand that, but the fact still remains. We need more output," the chief engineer said.

"How long before Grannalt is able to check things out and weigh in?" Another scientist asked.

"Give him some time. He was already too weak to even be in the testing lab, let alone operating the cannon. Maybe in a few days," the senior advisor replied.

"Well, we've waited this long. A few more won't kill us."

The senior advisor sat in a chair next to the queen-sized bed where Grannalt lay sleeping peacefully. He watched the alien's chest slowly rise and fall with each soft breath. Dark circles shaded the lower eyelids and his skin was paler than usual. His body had healed within three days but he was still too weak to move. The senior advisor leaned forward and swept a few stray hairs from Grannalt's face.

He had been given a proper bath and a gentle massage to alleviate some of the tension. A hair cut was done turning the tangled mess down his back into a more manageable length just below his shoulder blades.

"How could they do this to you?"

A soft rapping at the door signaled one of the orderlies who took care of him over the years coming in. The man had deep regret etched in his facial features knowing he couldn't atone for it. He should have thought about that instead of letting it all happen and joining in on the festivities, Senior advisor thought to himself. There was no excuse for anyone to go along with it, himself included.

"I just need to check his vitals and I'll be on my way," the orderly stated.

"You do that." Senior Advisor did not hide his contempt.

When the orderly was done and left the room, the senior advisor stood up placing a hand on Grannalt's.

"I will find out where they took your children. Please be patient with me." He walked out of the sparsely furnished bedroom and headed to his office. There were a few leads he had to dig into.

⌒

Darnizva paced the entire space of his living quarters for a good twenty minutes before Sspark came barging in unannounced, again spoiling his thought process. To this day, he still could not fathom why his father mated with the flamboyant little snot. He halted his steps and waited for whatever revelation Sspark was about to spew.

"Did you see that pitiful cannon shot from Earth's surface?"

"It's a great achievement in only ten years' time. Don't mock them."

"Hardly. What do they plan to do with such a thing? There's no way it can cripple, let alone shoot down, a Relliant ship."

"We may have to build it for them."

Darnizva sat on the cushioned window seat, Sspark plopping down beside him. The sparkly silver hair sprawling around Sspark's shoulders caught the light. Darnizva clamped his mouth shut before he said something cruel.

"Really?" Sspark drawled.

"I think it's only fair since we didn't even bother to find an uninhabited place to jump. Granted, we were in the middle of a brutal fight."

"You've grown very fond of this species."

"I do have offspring there, or have you forgotten?"

"I'd forgotten."

Sspark leaned forward to adjust a boot and Darnizva noticed the lieutenant was in female form. He glanced at that body and his lips pursed into a straight line. It was always hard to tell when Sspark was in either stage because even as a female, there wasn't much endowment. One thing was indisputable; Sspark was strikingly beautiful.

"I really do need help with this. I am the one who pulled the ships from the front lines into the jump." If Sspark was listening it didn't register.

"Fine. You can have two of my engineers."

"Interfacers?" Darnizva asked, hopeful.

"Yes, yes. Interfacers. You can't get much done without one, now can you?"

"I may start to like you, Lieutenant."

"Stop joking. You hate me more than you hate your father."

"That's not true. I resent you saying it."

Sspark straightened up from messing with the boot and stared into his eyes. "Then you're a fool. I would get rid of you in a heartbeat if I had a chance and could get away with it."

"No, you wouldn't."

"I have to go. You're not being any fun today."

Sspark rose from the window seat and exited out the chamber.

"Thank you!" Darnizva called out before the door slid shut.

∽

General Hoskins screamed internally watching Darnizva introduce the two aliens he brought with him. The General had come in person with some of the best weapons specialists on the planet to get some work done on the cannon and found not only that lab rat Professor Lancaster kept alive, but this little surprise.

This is not what I wanted!

Compared to the other soldiers of their race, the two Karysilan engineers were short, standing at around five feet eleven inches tall. One had dark red wavy hair cropped short and wore a black ensemble that did not flatter him. The other one was a bit taller with dark shoulder length hair and piercing amber colored eyes.

"I have brought two special engineers with me, courtesy of Lieutenant Sspark. They are known as Interfacers and can navigate through any system."

"So, they're just some hippie hackers?" Hoskins snorted.

"Hmm maybe a little more than that." He gestured to the main console of the cannon and the two went up to it. "Tell me what you think."

Long thin tendrils exuded from their bodies and wormed their way into the console. The Interfacers' eyes glowed and the main units sprang to life.

"Ugh!" The dark haired one exclaimed, leaning over as if he was ill. "Heavy, clunky, archaic. This life form running in the background, what is it?"

"You mean, the AI?" A scientist quipped.

"AI?"

"Artificial Intelligence. She is a system created to maintain the workings involved with the facility. She can always access the cannon should an incident occur."

"Warning! Unknown entity has infiltrated the main cannon controls." The AI's voice boomed from the communication speakers.

"She doesn't seem to like it when we go searching," the red haired one said.

"Is it okay if we shut her down for a while until we figure out some things?" The dark haired one asked.

"What?" Hoskins exploded. "You can't let them just go in and monkey with our systems! We have security measures to adhere to!"

"Calm down, General. I assure you everything will be fine." The senior advisor sounded like he was cooing at him, which infuriated him more. "Isn't that right, Grannalt?"

Grannalt stopped dead in his tracks seeing Captain Darnizva standing in the middle of the lab. He wasn't sure what to do, being in the same room as his own race after so long. Speechless, he only nodded.

Darnizva walked over to Grannalt and placed his hands against the young soldier's face.

"We will win this battle and then we can go home, if you like. But, I need you to help me with this planet's defense. Can you do that for me?" He watched the tears fill his eyes. "Whatever you have been through is over now. I need you to obey my order."

"Yes, Captain." Grannalt managed to breathe out.

"Good. Disable her. You can bring her back online when we're done."

"Of course, Captain."

"By the way," Darnizva added as he walked back to

the center of the lab, "You did a great job of creating her considering you are not a technician or an engineer."

"Warning! Imminent danger to main systems grid." The AI sounded desperate.

"That being said, hurry up and shut her down. She's starting to annoy me." The dark haired one commanded. His eyes flickered.

"Yes sir."

Grannalt went to the terminal and manually disable the AI.

"Done."

"Thank you, soldier." To the red headed he said, "Let's dive."

Hoskins went up to the senior advisor and with gritted teeth made his feelings known.

"This is unacceptable! We are responsible for own destiny here. Helping out is one thing. It's another when they inject themselves into our business."

"I'm confused, General. Do you not want us to win this battle?"

"This battle is between humans and that nut job's little armada…"

"Command Fleet." Darnizva corrected him.

"…or command fleet, whatever. We don't have any agreement with these aliens! We can't trust them," he seethed. A deafening silence filled the room and Hoskins knew he had said too much.

"Well, that was enlightening." Darnizva folded his arms across his chest.

"Indeed." From the hallway came a voice Hoskins didn't think he would hear. General Perrara strode in like a white knight, his dress blues clean and crisp, and each medal glinting in the light. "Why do you look surprised to see me, General. Didn't I tell you I was going to be present for the next test fire?"

MAQUEL A. JACOB

"We haven't gone in and done our discoveries yet."

"No need," the dark haired Interfacer interjected.

"We have found the issue."

"And what is that?" Hoskins spat out.

"The new mineral created does not have the capacity to hold the amount of energy necessary and it will not withstand more than three shots."

"Then what do you suppose we use then?" Hoskins yelled.

"Ours."

The two engineers and Darnizva replied in unison.

Hoskins' head snapped back at the verbal assault. He felt his authority slipping through his fingers and he didn't like that at all.

I'll teach them something.

General Perrara watched Hoskins with deep suspicion. Ever since military forces worldwide joined to create a new super power, the man had been sore about it. Contrary to what Hoskins thought, America could no longer be called one. The man was delusional and could not fathom the reality that their battle against an unknown alien race factored into their survival. He could see the wheels turning in General Hoskins' twisted mind from across the room.

"When you say yours," Perrara asked.

"We have a similar mineral that we use for our fighter ships' drive. If harnessed correctly, your output would increase by at least eighty percent," the red-haired engineer explained. "It's quite primitive, but I believe it will be very beneficial to you."

"Well, we are advancing as fast as we can, technology wise." Perrara noticed Hoskins was not listening to a word anyone was saying. "If it is successful, how many cannons would we need to cover our asses?"

The dark-haired engineer frowned, thinking.

Darnizva answered first.

"I think eight would suffice. Four in the center and one at each interval around the planet." He looked up at the giant boulder of mineral floating in the cannons reservoir. "And, our mineral would only be a third of the size."

"Good to know." Out of the corner of his eye, Perrara saw Hoskins excuse himself and leave the laboratory. "Just out of curiosity, how well have you fared with the Relliants in your battles?"

"Hard to say. We have been at war with them for centuries. Our loss and victories are about equal. In your terms, like civil war."

"Ahh, I understand now."

"But, they are quite ruthless. Possibly due to them being a primarily pure race."

"Pure?"

"Their level of interbreeding with other species is practically zero."

"And Karysilan?"

"We are made up of different hybrids of races but live on our planet together in peace. No race has ever tried to invade or destroy it."

"Not even the Relliants?"

Perrara was by far intrigued.

"No. I feel it is because of our mix that we are left alone. You've seen Lieutenant Zanzibar?"

"Of course."

"He is half Relliant and something else."

"What else?"

"We're not sure, but maybe one of the Unknown."

"Now I'm confused, Captain."

"The Unknowns are a hive race. They think and move as one and are considered a great force to behold.

In essence, steer clear if possible."

"So many races. You do realize how mind boggling this is to humans? Many of us didn't feel there were other carbon-based life forms outside our solar system."

"After over a half a century on your planet, I understand full well. But the fact remains, there are thousands of other races and species that exist."

An idea popped into General Perrara's mind and he knew Professor Makoto would be on board. The possibilities were endless. The two Interfacers were hard at work tweaking the cannon, the tiny feelers repositioning themselves often. He had another epiphany just watching them.

"As far as the training sessions, how difficult would it be to get some of the others to teach their race's fighting techniques?"

"You mean, bring other Karysilans here?"

"Yes," General Perrara's eyes gleamed.

"Hmm. It would take about five years for them to arrive through a jump, but it is doable."

"With about thirty-five years to spare."

"Why do you ask?" Darnizva seemed suspicious.

"I figure, if we are going to fight head to head with the Relliants, it would be in our best interest to just do it right and learn everything we can."

"You seem to have a better grasp on the situation than General Hoskins," Darnizva commented.

General Perrara gave a tiny smile. "I do." Grabbing his hat from under his armpit, he nodded. "I have some errands to attend to. I look forward to our collaboration." As he left the laboratory he caught a glimpse of General Hoskins talking in wild animation into the commlink attached to his ear.

Oh, dear God have mercy on us all.

A BEAUTIFUL UGLY MESS

Every scientist, engineer and technician in the room stared wide eyed at what they had created in only ten months' time. The observation officers had tracked down in secret the Relliant ship sitting just outside Alpha Centauri's orbit. General Hoskins' plan which entailed using something akin to a planet bomb to destroy it was underway. He figured by eliminating the ship, the Relliants would not have time to call for reinforcements, referring to it as 'nipping the issue in the ass'.

A great achievement was made yet the workers felt morally and ethically filthy. Whether they should have done it was never considered. The orders came down and there was no choice in the matter. Some scientists working on the project had died horribly while manipulating the stolen alien technology. It was essentially an H bomb but one hundred times deadlier with a new delivery system created for reaching its target faster.

General Hoskins smiled proudly at his new toy, clasping the rails of the observation deck with excitement. No more pussy footing around waiting for an alien attack. You hit your enemy first before they got the upper hand. He saw the grim faces surrounding him and felt a twinge of anger.

"What the hell's the matter with all of you? We're about to stop this damn war in its tracks before it even starts. You should hold be proud." Some stared at him in awed disbelief. "You're Americans, for God's sake. Show some pride!" He added.

Small rounds of golf claps went through the chamber, lack luster and filled with despair. He knew they were all tired from being worked to the bone, but it was not over yet. They still had to launch the damn thing. All the world leaders would be quite surprised and feel silly for not thinking about this sooner. This is what went through his head as he headed to the command center to see how preparations were going.

"What, the living fuck, is that?"

The newly appointed President of the United States asked this while pointing up at the giant center vidscreen showing the image of a projectile heading towards Alpha Centauri. The words were vulgar, immature and wholly un-presidential. At age thirty-seven, he was one of the youngest presidents in U.S. history. The previous president had bowed out of his duties after eight years even though elections had screeched to a halt after the aliens showed themselves. In general, the people of Earth didn't want too many hands in the pot for the next fifty years.

His advisors were all on their commlinks trying to figure out just that. The left vidscreen flickered on and Commander Ammordia's face loomed down on them.

"What have you done?" She demanded.

"I didn't do anything!" The President snapped.

"Where is it coming from?" He bellowed at his advisors.

"I can tell you exactly where it came from," Ammordia answered. Everyone stopped what they were doing and stared up into her image. "The continent of the United States."

"Oh, my God," one of the advisors blurted out as he

held his commlink to his ear and turned to the president. "She's right."

"Every world dignitary is up in arms and about to declare war for this travesty," his Vice President remarked as she too listened to her ear piece shaking her head. Her caramel brown skin was flushed with shades of red.

"How?" President whispered.

"I can tell you, the Relliant's general will not take this lightly. Whoever did this has assured your race's extinction. We can assist but our fleet is only one of hundreds in our military."

"Can you stop it?" President asked her.

"We wouldn't make it in time. As powerful as that weapon may be in your eyes, it will probably not put much of a dent in a Relliant ship's hull. If it does, then kudos to you for advancing in your last hours."

"Who did this?" President shouted.

His face was beet red and his body visibly shook. Secretary Regis was afraid he was on the verge of a nervous breakdown at his fairly young age.

General Perrara burst into the situation room and seeing the president in such a state, cursed not just Hoskins, but himself for not putting a leash on that dog earlier. His usually pristine attire was ruffled from double timing it as fast as his convoy would allow.

"President, sir," he exclaimed, out of breath. The man looked up at him. "Hoskins," was all Perrara said and the president's eyes opened wider. A kind of rage he had never witnessed in another human's face was displayed for all to see. The screen above continued to show the missile's silent travel as it carried the most destructive bomb ever created by human hands towards the enemy ship.

Ammordia's gaze shifted to Darnizva entering the room. Upon hearing General Hoskins name, he made a face she had not seen before either. A mixture of pain and defeat that was not flattering.

"So, he has plunged humanity into the depths of hell out of his own stupidity." Darnizva managed to speak through tight lips.

"Get him on screen! Now!" The President ordered.

Communications personnel scrambled to the task, themselves feeling angry and helpless. Within minutes, the vidscreen on the right lit up and General Hoskins' smug face appeared. The President and General Perrara went slacked jawed at his audacity to be proud of the disaster.

"General! You better explain this!"

"Of course, Mr. President. Please calm yourself," Hoskins said in a soothing voice. "This is a great step for us to prevent this war from even happening. Striking first is the best course of action. I'm surprised none of my colleagues had considered this." He eyed General Perrara who looked at him as if he were crazed.

"What you have done is get our entire race, and our planet, annihilated in one fell swoop!" The President was having a hard time containing his anger.

"Once the enemy ship is destroyed, we will be in the clear. They won't have time to call for help."

"You stupid, insane human," Ammordia spat.

"How long before it reaches the ship?" Secretary Regis inquired the tracking specialist.

"At the speed it's going, two hours."

"Oh my God," Vice President grabbed her midsection and keeled over to her knees. "There's no time to warn or save anyone."

"What is wrong with you all?" General Hoskins taunted. "We're not doomed. This is a preemptive strike to save our race. I did the only right thing in our situation."

"You better hope we all die here in the next few hours, because if we don't, I will have your ass on a stick!" The President, still shaking with rage, pointed a finger at Hoskins' image. "Turn him off!"

The vidscreen went blank, cutting Hoskins off before he could reply. Ammordia shook her head in disbelief while Darnizva began to pace the floor along with everyone else. One could feel the nervous tension all around. They watched in silence as the missile got closer to its target and ports opened on the Relliant ship revealing the angry glow of their weapons bays.

"Incoming message, sir!"

The communications officer announced.

"From where?" Just as he asked, he knew. "Relliant ship, sir."

"Put it on screen."

The President suddenly felt extremely tired.

The Relliant general's face appeared on the screen and he was not smiling. Behind him, soldiers rushed to man stations and the background lit up from consoles coming to life.

"Was I wrong in being generous and giving you time, albeit a short fifty years, to prepare? Is this your answer?"

"I assure you, this was not planned by me or any of the world leaders."

"Assure me?"

His image disappeared and was replaced by his ship's radar tracking the missile. He returned with a defiant look.

"Why should I believe you? I think a lesson in power needs to be demonstrated from my end as well, don't you agree?"

The vidscreen went blank and so did the President's eyes. His body swayed as his legs began to falter. One of his advisors caught him before he hit the floor. Without any orders, three assistants went to get the medical doctor.

"I have to consult the General," Ammordia blurted and the vidscreen cut out.

"We have to warn the people," the Press Secretary pleaded.

"And say what?" Vice President inquired. "We have less than two hours before our entire planet is destroyed and our race extinct? I don't want to hear that on my commute."

"It would be over in moments," Darnizva concluded.

Everyone just stood watching the scene play out as the Reliant ship fired a stream of red glowing orbs towards the bomb and planet Earth. Some fell to their knees and cried, others were in a state of shock.

Doom was near.

From the corner of the screen, a large vortex appeared on the side between the Relliant ship and the missile. A bright beam of light shot forth out of its gaping whirlwind and hit the barrage of Relliant rounds and the missile dead on. The vidscreen lit up from the blast and the image was blown out in a flash of white. When it cleared, they could all see a large organic looking ship emerge from the center of the vortex and position itself in front of the Relliant ship, blocking its ports.

On both the Karysilan and Relliant ships as well as inside the situation room, the image of space was replaced by a male with long dark hair and fluorescent green eyes. He smiled beautifully but something was not quite right about it.

"General Tartha, you must keep your promises. It would not look good in the eyes of your race. Your father should have taught you that." His voice was like honey.

Again, that smile surfaced.

"Why?" Darnizva whispered in horror as he took in the newcomer's face and surroundings in the background of the transmission.

"What's wrong?" The President whipped around at him, also whispering. He was sure they had just been miraculously saved but the Captain did not look happy to see their savior. On the other vidscreen, Relliant General Tartha appeared and he too looked visibly shaken.

"This has nothing to do with your kind!" Tartha shrieked. His voice warbled as he tried to sound authoritative.

"Oh?" Their savior replied. "Like you, I am also curious about these humans. You must learn to share." He turned his attention to Darnizva and smiled sweetly. "Don't mind us. We are just here to observe and reap the spoils when it's over."

"Did he just refer to himself in plural?" The President asked in a hushed tone.

"Because he is part of a whole." Darnizva answered.

The President paled. "Are these the Unknowns?"

"No." Darnizva said flatly. "Something much worse." He turned to the President. "Organics."

"Say what?

"That's the only way to explain them."

"I don't really like that term, Captain." The smiling male beauty jumped in. "I'd like to think we are just more capable of evolving or devolving to match our situations."

As he sat back in his seat, his hands and part of his lower body were revealed. Someone in the room gagged at what resembled clumps of raw meat, the long robe and cloak unable to hide it, making for a mismatched sight.

"I will not let you interfere with their progress, Tartha. You will have a fair battle as planned in the agreed upon time." He tilted his head to one side and addressed the humans. "I am Cresnia, the entity that operates this ship and guardian of everything aboard it." Cresnia straightened his head and smiled again, this time his creepiness not in doubt. "I look forward to knowing more about your kind."

Once Cresnia's image disappeared, General Tartha leaned into the screen and declared, "If I see another attempt like this, I don't care what that monster says. I will not be mocked!" He too disconnected his link and the transmission ended.

"We were just saved, right?"

Secretary Regis asked softly.

"Yeah," the President dragged out the word.

"Then, why are we not cheering?"

"Because…. why?" He asked Darnizva.

"Organics have factories on their ships that take the bodies of other races and reconfigure them to be automaton soldiers."

"I think I'm going to be ill," the Vice President spoke.

General Perrara regained his posture and straightened out his uniform the best he could. The Press Secretary gave him a quizzical look.

"As much as I would like to rejoice that we were just saved from annihilation by something even worse, I feel General Hoskins may think he is in the clear on this one."

He smoothed his hair back with his hands and patted the sides for good measure.

The President's cheeks went red. He wanted to kill Hoskins himself but knew there was no way his advisors would let him do it.

"We know what you're thinking, sir, and believe me when I tell you, none of us would raise a finger to stop you," his head assistant said.

"But I will," Secretary Regis interjected. "IF it needs to be done, I will handle it…discreetly. You must have plausible deniability, sir."

"On that note," Darnizva moved towards the door. "My people must figure out how to keep that thing away of your dearly departed in the future." A few advisors shuddered. "I will be in touch." He turned and left.

A deep silence ensued, everyone seeming breathless and not daring to move. Doom had been averted, but at a heavy price. They were now indebted to a race of fiends. No one felt celebratory. The jarring sounds of international commlinks springing to life with shouts of elation snapped them out of it and the President mentally prepared for the task of breaking the news to the world dignitaries; gently.

General Hoskins watched the footage from his own situation room located deep in a bunker and waited patiently for the bomb to make impact until he saw the Relliant ship's weapons bays open. He had been in his share of fire fights so seeing the trajectory of the shots let him know how much he had miscalculated the enemy. His body stiffened and he paled when the organic ship appeared and wiped out the Relliant's weapons along with his prized missile in one shot.

The vidscreen shifted and he saw Cresnia. He heard every word but said nothing when the transmission ended. His staff was waiting with bated breath for his instructions but he had none. Not only had the mission failed due to outside interference, there was now a new threat to his agenda.

Even before the commlink signaled an incoming message from the President and the vidscreen came back to life, General Hoskins had fled, heading towards the rendezvous point he had designated with his trusted team in case of failure. He knew his position was in jeopardy and needed to act quickly with plan B.

Training Sessions

Geoffrey Hagen saw his work cut out for him in regards to getting his soldiers back on track. Six hours into combat maneuvers and nearly all of them were drenched in sweat from fatigue, barely making their marks. After arriving on Earth, he made sure to increase his status in the world so he could build the training facility. It was imperative to have means to keep the soldiers and himself in top form.

Since that preposterous reveal years ago, many Relliant operatives had come out of hiding and, much to his chagrin, out of shape. He shook his head in disgrace at the lackluster efforts of the newcomers. Lieutenants Bree and Craig were faring better than most but not anywhere close to expectations. Both had labored breathing and he could see the muscles in their body twitch from overexertion. If this were a real battlefield, where the fighting could easily last twenty hours, they would all be dead.

"Enough!" He roared. "Drop your weapons!" Some struggled with the order, an attempt to convey they're capability of continuing, but he was not going to have that. "If all weapons are not on the ground in five seconds, I will come and strike you down myself." He unfolded his arms and took a step forward and landed one foot on the first stair. A loud series of thuds and clanking resonated as every soldier did what they were told out of fear.

Hagen continued his descent and a gust of wind whipped through the canyon, forcing his long dark hair and black cloak straight back behind him. Dressed in a full black leather body tunic with black boots, he was the epitome of a nemesis. Standing on the ground, he observed his soldiers and then let out a long exhale.

"I know this is hard for some of you because you have been sitting on your asses indulging in human interaction instead of acting like the Relliant warriors that you are, but that is no excuse for such poor performance. I am deeply disappointed." Heads hung in shame, they didn't even look up at him. "Get some rest. We will continue in twelve hours. Bree, Craig." He motioned for them to follow.

Tired yet perfectly erect in posture, Bree strode behind him. Craig was breathing loudly trying to catch his breath and stumbled after them. When it came to strength and ability, Bree won hands down. As great a fighter Craig was, he could never match his mate. Hagen watched him get infuriated and jealous at Bree's stamina.

In his private chamber, Hagen had them sit on the lounge sofa while an attendant brought muscle relaxant packs and ice water. Bree sipped, applying the packs at major pinpoints. Craig, in contrast, gulped down two glasses before slapping packs on every place that hurt.

How did they ever become mates? Hagen wondered.

He removed his cloak and sat in a plush oversize chair across from them.

"I don't have to tell you how important it is that my two seconds in command should be the elite so far. What are your thoughts on what needs attention for you to get back to your old selves?"

"I need to work on my agility and gain some muscle

mass. Right now, I have very little of that and body fat."

"You have never had much body fat," Hagen tsked. "But I do agree on the other two." He turned to Craig, who guzzled another glass of water and barely choked it down.

Craig looked up, saw Hagen staring at him and nodded his head while tapping his chest. Clearing his throat, he also replied.

"I believe I need to have more endurance and stamina. It's not so much tiring as it is I am running out of energy too fast."

"Agreed." Crossing his legs and leaning back into the chair he added, "And?"

Both soldiers stared at him in confusion and then looked at each other. Finally, Bree answered him.

"We need to spar with our officers, not our lower ranked soldiers." Hagen nodded and tilted his head. "And with each other."

"Correct. I will also contribute to your training."

Hagen smiled.

"Can we wait on that?" Craig reared back holding up one hand in a stop motion.

Hagen narrowed his eyes at his remark. Leave it to Craig to try and find a way out of something, even if it was beneficial to him. Bree's lips tightened into a thin line of exasperation but he did not speak. His ability to assess the situation and hold back was something Hagen admired about the young commander.

"Let's not." Dejected, Craig went silent. "Now, both of you rest. I have other errands to run." Hagen stood, donning his cloak. This time securing it around his waist with a wide belt.

"You want us to rest here? In your chamber?"

"Why would I permit you to leave when neither one of you can barely move?"

"Craig," was all Bree said, stopping another word from coming out of his mouth.

"Make sure you are back on the training grounds at the deadline."

"Yes, Commander!" They both replied in unison as he exited the room.

~

Sspark casually strode from one end of the training arena to the other, patiently waiting for all the chosen participants to line up. One of the football stadiums had been decommissioned then reconfigured for combat maneuvers. Casing the perimeter, Sspark felt it too constraint. He would have to dial down his power by at least fifty percent so the entire place didn't get obliterated.

"It's that fucking crazy killer from that broadcast years ago," he heard one of the American soldiers say to his comrade in not so soft a voice. Loud hushes erupted as the soldier was reprimanded verbally, thinking Sspark was not in ear shot on the other side.

"I can hear at a much higher level than humans, so," he stopped his stroll, pivoted and came up to the soldier like a bullet. A gust of wind came a few seconds behind him. He stared down into the soldier's fear-stricken face. At six feet four inches tall, Sspark was considered short for his race, but he made up for it in strength. "Yes, I am that crazy killer." He smiled, showing all teeth as the soldier's crotch darkened. Urine seeped down onto the turf. Tears streaked the man's cheeks but he didn't move, staying at attention.

General Perrrara, along with other world military leaders, took his seat in the bleachers section across from the soldiers. This gave them a great vantage point to see the action. Darnizva had assured him that there would be no casualties this time. Witnessing the interaction between the soldier and Sspark, he had his doubt. This may be a promise no one would be able to keep.

"Are we all here, then?" Sspark asked politely. "Good. I am Lieutenant Sspark of the League and a wielder of the Sphere." He bowed graciously.

"What does that even mean?" The general from Italy shrugged while asking.

Darnizva stepped out of the shadows and onto the Astroturf, stealing Sspark's moment.

"There is a core that resides in its own solar system with two moons. It grants portions of its power to a select few throughout the universe. Right now, only a mere eight hundred individuals in the galaxy have it. They can manifest it in different ways depending on the personality of the wielder."

Sspark frowned. He could not have explained it better and Darnizva knew that. He was going to add his own flare of over exaggeration knowing it would put many of the humans off. Admitting defeat for now, Sspark raised his head, returning a sickening sweet smile Darnizva's way.

"Which makes me extremely special, don't you think?" He saw the color drain from the military leaders' faces and felt a sense of accomplishment. "Well, let's get to it, shall we?" Sspark summoned his Sphere. When it solidified into the silver metallic staff, glinting in the light, he prodded, "So, who would like to come first?"

The lesson was short lived as thirty soldiers charged him and he knocked them away with a series of whirlwind swings, sending them all flying backwards fifty feet in the air. Some landing badly and bones could be heard breaking on impact. Two hundred and twenty soldiers stood at ease still in formation watching the scene unfold.

MAQUEL A. JACOB

"How stupid," Sspark commented. "I was obviously joking. Did you really think an attack in numbers would bring me down?" He threw back his head and laughed at the sky. Returning his gaze to the ones still standing he made an announcement. "For those of you who know better, I have a gift for you. Real training."

A medical unit on standby rushed into the arena to gather up and remove the injured. It took less than ten minutes and Sspark marveled at their efficiency. Once they were done, he resumed his speech, eyeing Darnizva to make sure he didn't interfere again.

"As you know, alien DNA was introduced into your bodies to give greater agility and speed. You are going to need both in this battle. Since your bodies will not know how to accommodate these new abilities, they will need to be calibrated. The exercises will be tedious, but by the end, you will be five times faster and more agile than you could have ever imagined."

Sspark put away his Sphere and moved from the center of the arena to the edge. Ten lines formed on the ground from one end to the other. A giant digital timer sat at each end along with a medical crew. He was going to do this in stages so the ones who were not first could watch in envy and anticipation. Nothing got a soldier more riled up than seeing what his fellow comrade could do and then vow to upstage them.

"I want the first fifty of you to head to the end." They obediently jogged down and positioned themselves five to a line. Sspark liked that. "First up, speed." He smiled, keeping his mouth closed. "I want you to run normally, like a sprint, to the other side. When you get there, I want you to run back, giving it a little more. This will be repeated ten times and recorded. Oh," he spun around before going to sit in the bleachers with the military leaders, "You will be blindfolded so you don't see your

216

results. We don't want you trying too hard."

The first three runs were impressive to the military leaders as each soldier reached Olympic record speeds, but after the seventh they sat stunned. Many of the soldiers began running at thirty-five to forty miles per hour. By the tenth and last run, some had hit the fifty miles per hour mark. Sspark was more interested in the eighty who were impatiently, seeing the potential that awaited them. He saw Darnizva shake his head in disapproval.

So what? Sspark snapped at him telepathically. It's not like he was inciting a riot.

"Thank you, soldiers. Please follow the medical team and head back to the locker rooms." A fresh medical team arrived on the empty side as the other filed out. The soldiers could barely walk straight and he knew why. Their bodies had yet to catch up with themselves. "Next fifty, please."

Despite not doing any combat maneuvers, Sspark was having fun observing the humans. The best part was the military leaders on the edge of their seats salivating at the results. This is only the beginning. Sspark chuckled in delight. Darnizva's face hardened.

Kevin Lang sat in front of his prisoner watching for any sign of consciousness. The two men had been playing peek-a-boo every time they were alone together. He and the General couldn't seem to get along these days, taking into consideration the roles they were in. A slight movement around the ears let him know the general was indeed awake.

"Really, General, let's not do this today. It's so tiring." He grabbed the ice bucket of water and tossed its contents into the general's face. The man shot upright and inhaled sharply. "See, that's better."

The General's eyes burned with hatred and Kevin understood that.

Over the course of his stay in Kevin's research lab, the general would not comply with simple instructions, thus drastic measures had been taken. Limbs and other appendages were severed only to be reattached later via a new medical system Kevin himself had devised with the help of Professor Morandi's scientists. The marks left were perfect lines on the general's body yet he could still feel the pain of it. It had been termed 'Phantom Trauma'.

"Why do you resist me so? You can't blame me for wanting to use you in my experiments after you came bursting in here, guns blazing, with every intent to do harm."

"You fucking monster."

The General spat at him and it landed mid-way.

"I have a new proposal." Kevin waited for the general to turn his head in defiance. "You help me take control of Hoskins' Terror squads and I let you work security detail at one of our facilities."

"Give up one of my fellow men to you and become some rent a cop for your organization? Fuck you!"

"Do you really want to be associated with him right now?" That got the general's attention. Kevin gestured towards the viewing window at one of the guards. "Load the footage on the tablet and bring it in."

A tall blond woman in white scrubs entered the cell carrying the device. She grabbed a chair on her way and sat down a few feet from the general. Turning the tablet so he could see the screen, she tapped a video icon and played the footage of what transpired between the Relliant ship and the missile.

"General Hoskins had been busy building some monstrosity of a bomb that he put inside a missile and sent hurling to the Relliant ship. As you can see, it failed.

General Hoskins is on a leave of absence pending review. No one can find him, yet."

The General's face stiffened, his eyes squeezed shut.

"Stupid!" He seethed quietly.

"Yes, indeed. Now, what do you think happened with his Terror squads?"

"He either snatched them all up or they are sitting in limbo."

"I would guess sitting in limbo since his headquarters would be the first place the President's men looked. You misunderstood me earlier. Running security at one of our facilities means watching over the Terrors once we transfer them."

"Why?"

"Hmm?"

"Why let me loose to run the Terrors? I could easily turn against you."

"And what makes you believe we would let you?" Kevin leaned forward. "Retaliation against us would not be in your best interest." The general hung his head real-izing the truth in his words. "General, all we ask is that you work with us. A little insight on the Terrors," Kevin said softly. "They can eliminate us any time they want. We just think we're controlling them when it's farther from the truth."

"Then…?"

"They have their own agenda and I, for one, would like to see it come to fruition."

"What kind of agenda?"

"An experiment in the human condition and a new kind of law enforcement geared towards justice for Bi- Genetics."

The general snorted.

"Justice. For those creatures?"

When he looked back up he went rigid and his eyes

went wide. Bound to the chair, he was unable to move back or defend himself.

Kevin had not moved but a ball of flames hovered above his head. His grey eyes seemed to turn into orbs of starlight. There was a storm raging behind those eyes and the general wanted no part of it.

"General," Kevin sighed heavily. "We really must discuss your attitude towards my kind. Now, should I burn you to a crisp and see if we can regenerate your entire body? Or, do we have an understanding?"

"Please," the general whispered. "Whatever you want."

"Good." The ball of flames dissipated to vapors and Kevin sat back against the chair. "Tell me about the Terrors and how to find them."

‿

A tumbleweed the size of a beach ball rolled across the makeshift road forcing the lead hummer to swerve around it. The other vehicles followed. As the first one reached the planned coordinates, the scenery shimmied as if a heat wave had come through and the hummer disappeared. The same happened with the others and a different landscape emerged ahead. All the vehicles stopped, their occupants exiting one by one to look up at the towering structure before them.

Sitting high above the valley, carved into the side of a mountain, the new Terror base gleamed silver from the sun's contact. Two rows of bay windows were visible from a few miles away and no entrance in sight. Surrounding the mountain was a sandy desert with hilly plains scattered about.

Inside the bay windows on the second tier of the mountain stood a lone figure staring down at the entourage of scientists gathered in a cluster. The building's entire upper level was stark white.

"How do we get in?" A scientist asked Kevin.

"That's a good question."

"Did you not stipulate that access was required when you handed this over and scheduled the inspection?"

"We didn't hand them the base, they built it themselves," Kevin retorted. He then spoke the code into his commlink and connected with security.

A familiar voice came crackling through.

"Ortega Base."

"General, how good to hear your voice."

A long silence followed then, "I do not comprehend the title. Please state your purpose."

Unnerved, Kevin cleared his throat. Something was not right. "To speak with the head of Ortega Base."

"Is the head aware of your visit?"

"I should say so, since he is staring right at us." Kevin waved at the man in the window, who nodded and turned to speak with someone behind him.

"Please wait for transport." The connection died.

Within twenty minutes a giant white aircraft, resembling a helicopter smashed flat to make room, came over the mountains and headed their way. The engines were barely audible and it hovered effortlessly before landing fifty feet away from the group. A tall man with dark hair and glowing purple eyes came out of the opened slide panel. His commlink appeared to be a part of his body as it slid from behind his ear and stopped near the corner of his mouth.

"Ready to transport the visitors," he spoke in a strange electronic voice that cut out in places. "Roger that." He replied to whoever was on the other end of the conversation.

Kevin took in the thing before him in its entirety and knew what the possibility was. For a new law enforcement to be create, beings unaffected by Bi-Genetic talents were needed. This resemblance of a man was the result. It motioned for them to enter the aircraft and they all obediently filed in.

It took off into the air not having to adjust for weight and glided back to the other side of the mountain, touching down on the landing pad atop the roof. Once everyone was out of the aircraft, they were ushered into an elevator built into the wall of the mountain. It shot down ten levels to the bay deck in three seconds causing a few in the group to hold back their lunch from involuntarily coming up. As it opened, they came within range of the figure who stared down at them in the desert.

Terence Young, formerly Terror Eight, stood straight with his hands clasped behind his back. His hair hung down in a ponytail to his waist and he wore a military style jacket rimmed with purple trim, black pants and boots. When he turned to acknowledge them, a slight smile formed. He looked dangerous.

"Kevin Lang. How nice of you to partake of my invitation."

"Of course. I was dying to know how you accomplished the first steps of your goal."

"Were you really?" Terence turned around fully and took in the group of scientists that accompanied Kevin. "Why bring them?"

"To observe, nothing more." Kevin responded feeling a sense of resentment from Terence just as he said it.

What are you hiding? Kevin spoke to him telepathically.

Nothing that the military hasn't done before. Was Terence's reply.

That doesn't make it right. Kevin snapped back.

Terence raised an eyebrow.

What have you done to the General?

Terence tapped his commlink.

"Security officer zero one zero, report to the main deck."

A moment later, what used to be a vibrant older man full of pride came marching in and Kevin stepped back in horror. Some of the scientist were confused until they realized who they were looking at. They too took a step away from it. Purple eyes glowed back at them and a tiny purple LED commlink protruded from behind his ear on the shaved side of his head.

"Why have you done this?" Kevin asked, filled with regret. He had promised the general safe haven while tending to the Terrors' wellbeing. This should not be.

"He would not comply to my demands so I had to recalibrate him to obey."

"He's not some machine!"

"No. He's better than that."

"How? Where did you learn something like this?"

Terence smiled wide this time.

"A little organic birdy came down to the Earth's surface and whispered it to me."

Kevin felt his stomach lurch unkindly.

Just watching for the show, my ass.

He knew then that the Organics had their own reasons for arriving into Earth space unannounced. Terence tilted his head, motioning for Kevin to come closer to the bay window. As he did, the windows became vidscreens. Each one showed a different terrain being cultivated by other former Terrors.

"I give you Ortega City, Metropolis. A network of five communities connected by a hub, this base."

"What are these for?" Kevin dreaded the answer.

"My experiment in the human condition, of course."

"How will this benefit the war?"

"The war? Nothing. We want no part of it."

"You can't not be a part of it, Terence! The whole planet is in danger!"

"Make no mistake, we will defend ourselves. Just

not for the greater good of humanity. You, of all people, know this better than most." Terence narrowed his eyes.

Kevin did not need to be reminded of his past. He knew full well how horrid Normals could be, but he also knew there were good ones too, like Professor Morandi.

A tingle in his head alerted him to Terence invading his mind and he snapped the entry shut.

"This still does not make it right."

"You go help save humanity in your way, and I will do so in mine." Terence turned back to face the group of scientists awkwardly waiting for instruction. "Let's not fight, shall we? Are we ready for a tour of the facility?" He led the way, his stride purposeful.

CHAPTER SIX

EXPOSURE

The President paced around the oval office and when he stopped in the middle of the room, all eyes were on him. He was contemplating a reckless deed and knew his advisors wouldn't like it. It came to him two nights ago after talking with the Karysilans about their role in assisting Earth and how many soldiers were needed. Rubbing his eyes with two fingers, he let out a long sigh then looked up.

"I have a proposal." Tablets raised to the advisors' chests ready for dictation. The Vice President had a dubious look on her face as did Secretary Regis. "Since we know there are other aliens on our planet and even some Karysilans still hiding, I think we should find each and every one of them." No hands moved.

"To what end, sir?" Regis asked.

"We need more information and it's better if we get it from the source."

"The public won't like that. And, the ones who would relish in it, you are giving them fuel for the fire," his Vice President added.

"I'm not out to harm them." The President sounded defensive.

"That may be but they may not see it that way."

"More importantly," Regis stepped forward, "How are you going to find them?"

"Believe it, or not, Professor Lancaster developed a device that can detect non-humans."

Both the Vice President and Regis reared their heads back in disgust. Leave it to that degenerate to create something he probably used to get more specimens for his research. The man knew no bounds.

"Can it be done discreetly?" Vice President inquired.

"I'm not sure, but I hope so," The President replied.

Off in the corner, one of the aides slowly backed out of the room and into the hallway. He walked briskly until reaching the midpoint and stopped. Looking around to make sure no one was near, he pulled an older model smart phone from his inside jacket pocket and dialed.

Hoskins, now living on a tight rope since being on leave, shoveled beef stew in his mouth and sat back to enjoy the flavors. Another thing he found Bi- Genetics good for was cooking. They could master anything if they put their minds to it. Loud buzzing caused him to rock back upright and frantically search for the source. Under his napkin he found the smart phone he carried in case of emergencies.

"Hoskins," he snapped.

"Sir, it's Jesse. From the White House."

"Oh?" Hoskins wiped his mouth with the napkin and pushed the plate away. "I'm listening."

"The President apparently has a device Professor Lancaster made that can detect non-humans. He plans to find them here on Earth and get more information about our chances."

"Is that so?"

"Him, the Vice and Regis want to keep it discreet."

"Really?" Hoskins chuckled. This made his day. "I'll have a small detail follow their sniffers and have a camera crew ready to expose those creatures when they come out."

"Sir, that would make them wonder how the news media found out. I can't lose my job here. You said you needed me here as your eyes and ears."

"Stop pissing yourself!" Hoskins rolled his eyes. "No one will know it was you. I have no intention of hiding the fact that I will be to blame."

"Oh, okay."

"Now get back in there before they get all suspicious."

"Yes sir."

The line went silent and Hoskins set the phone face down on the table. He had a sinister smile as he reveled in the thought of messing up the President's plans. That sapling was not who Hoskins had wanted in the President's role so he didn't consider him as his commander in chief. Pulling his plate back closer to him, he waved for his assistant to join him. They had a bit of planning to do.

"Is this where I think we are?" one of the media crewmen asked as he stared up at the sign splayed across the building. It read:

YOUNG & TANNER AGENCIES

"Yep," the cameraman replied. "This is the house of supermodel elites."

"You can't be serious? One of them is an alien?" The man shrieked.

"Lower your voice!" the interviewer hissed. He had gotten the tip, along with other media groups about the President's plan. So far there were five crews in place at different locations. He rubbed his nose and sniffed. He didn't like the President trying to hide things from the American people. "The secret service guys are coming out with the package."

The front double doors opened and two men in black suits, white shirts and sunglasses stepped over the threshold. Two more were behind but in between them was the prize. Long lean legs the color of caramel walked out and as the crew's eyes traveled up, they saw the light brown mini skirt, wrap around top accented with a simple gold necklace and the face of a goddess.

At six feet three inches tall, super model Antona, was a beauty to be reckoned with. Her strawberry brown hair flowed down her back and the front of her shoulders. Eyes the color of the sea shone brightly before she pushed a pair of designer sunglasses on her face. Wearing a camel colored trench coat, the entire ensemble blended with her in every way.

Shaking off his feeling of being stunned, the interviewer made a circling motion with his hands signaling the crew. It was show time.

In the center of New York, Geoffrey Hagen, opera singer extraordinaire, was ambushed coming out of rehearsal for his upcoming show in two weeks. Movement out of the corner of his eye made him pause. He saw the shiny black sedans screech to a halt, surrounding him, and could not understand why so he stayed still. Not even a minute later, a cameraman came running up, an anchor woman and sound guy in tow. The secret service and a news crew? Hagen had a feeling this was not going to be good. The first question out of the anchor woman's mouth solidified it.

"Is it true that you are an alien? How long have you been here? Are you with the enemy?"

Secret service agents blocked their advance and pushed them back while four others grabbed Hagen and shoved him in one of the black sedans. It sped off, tossing

Hagen backwards further in the seat. He was not thrilled by these events and knew his two lieutenants were next.

The after party for the Academy award winning actor's new film release was being held at a night club on the outskirts of Miami where only those with lots of credit could enter. Surrounded by women, body guards and loud music, he didn't notice the secret service agents until they were a mere ten feet away from him. Looking up he saw their serious faces and contemplated running but he thought better of it. There was no reason for the secret service to be after him. His manager came around and squeezed himself between the agents and his client.

"Gentlemen! Can I help you with something?" His agent yelled over the loud techno music. All he received were stares as the men removed their glasses.

"Step aside. This is a matter of national security."

"What does that even mean? He's an actor for Christ's sake!"

The first one drew his weapon and the agent put both his hands up and backed off. He gave his client a shocked look and mouthed, What have you done?

"Mr. Chasner, if you would please come with us."

"Sure, man. Not a problem." He disengaged himself from the blanket of women and stood up towering over the two agents at six feet eight inches tall. The faux fur lined lapel coat he wore looked like it could be used as a blanket for a normal sized person. His hair was a dirty blonde that resembled a lion's mane filling the air around his head.

Walking past his agent he lifted a hand to say, 'be cool'. Then he put up his thumb and pinky, waving them as a sign that he would call when he could. People parted like the red sea as he was escorted outside the building into the bright street lights shining across the parking lot. The moment his eyes adjusted, all hell broke loose as reporters clamored towards him. He realized some of the bright lights came from camera mounts.

"Are you really an alien? What planet are you from? Do you fight for the enemy?"

The questions kept coming and he stood in a state of confusion until the agents yanked him to the side and forced him into a black sedan. He didn't have time to get situated, the vehicle pulling off with a loud screech, burning rubber on the pavement.

"What the hell is going on?" He snapped.

No one answered him.

"How did this happen?" The President yelled.

His entire advisory team along with his cabinet members were in the situation room with various shades of horror on their faces at the media nightmare unfolding on the telescreen. One of the aides came up to him and tapped his shoulder.

"You're not going to like this, sir."

"Just tell me," he retorted.

"It was Hoskins, sir. He's pulling the media's strings on this one."

The President blanched. Turning away slowly he reached the end of the operations console and swept everything off with one arm. He let out a loud roaring scream and banged his fists on the empty surface. Realizing how he had just conducted himself in front of his people, he straightened up and fixed his hair. Clearing his throat, he spoke.

"I want," he stretched his neck and cracked it, "you to find that son of a bitch. Even if it means scouring the corners of the Earth." He met everyone's gaze. "Are we on the same page?"

"Yes sir!"

The occupants of the room replied in unison.

"Good. Now, let's get the rest of them, discreetly. I want a security detail and," he raised a finger, "I want the media on a leash."

"It's too late for the next extraction, but we can be ready for the rest." Regis assured him.

Jesse felt unease in the pit of his stomach. He couldn't figure out why his loyalty to his boss made him feel this way lately. Was what he did wrong? Feeling eyes on him he looked to his right and saw one of Secretary Regis' assistants staring at him with contempt.

"Excuse me," he whispered, going around the assistant to the water tray. His throat was dry as the desert. He could feel her eyes follow him.

Craig's first reaction to seeing men in suits with guns was to get ready for combat. Fortunately, Bree stopped him and pulled him back by the bottom of his leather jacket. The scene was something out of a movie. Bree guessed it had something to do with their race. That they had been found out somehow. But, until it was confirmed, he planned to play stupid.

The agents had come in like gang busters not asking for cooperation from the security guards of the venue. Hence, the bouncers and road crew tried to stop their advance backstage. Bloody noses and cracked ribs were the result and everyone knew the agents meant business. The door slamming open and agents blocking the entryway is what caused Craig to start up.

"Breeton Mullens, Craig Otts, please accompany us. The President would like a word with you." The one on the left spoke.

Bree stood up and tugged Craig, who glanced at him incredulous, to follow. There was no reason to start a fight and further expose themselves if his guess was correct. He wondered if their commander was alright. The two agents didn't look too friendly and he assumed they were not going to be to anyone they capture.

Outside the room, four more agents were waiting to escort them out. A black sedan waited just on the edge of the back entrance leaving very little room for anyone to get between it and the small entourage. That didn't stop a mob of paparazzi from trying as they fired off questions about aliens and the enemy threat while snapping photos. Bree's suspicions were confirmed.

～

We might as well make a camp in this thing.

The President thought as he sat in a chair at the end of the long table in the situation room. As large as the place was, it felt cramped lately with all his people running around trying to keep everything under control. His legs were propped up on the table's edge and he fingered the hardcopy list of aliens found so far. This went beyond infiltration, in his book.

"How is it," he started, "That everyone we've found is a celebrity or in some high status of society?" He asked no one in particular. The aides nearest to him stopped what they were doing. "I mean, Christ! One of them is a famous opera singer who used to be a rock star."

"It seems they can adapt to any situation." Regis answered him. "It shouldn't be a surprise since we know Bi-Genetics can soak up all kinds of knowledge and become experts if they so choose."

"When is Darnizva scheduled to arrive?"

"He is running a bit late due to his task of sheltering his children who he fathered with humans."

"Oh, God! That's right! He does have half human kids." The President rubbed his eyes. "This is getting more complicated than I thought it would be."

One of Regis' assistants came up the two stairs into the cul de sac where the table sat. Her skirt suit was impeccable and not a hair out of place.

Where does Regis find these women?

"Sir, the conference room is prepped and no one is granted access except the ones you yourself authorized. For now, we have seven aliens waiting there. It was decided the best way to interview them would be in small groups."

"Thank you," he paused.

"Tanisha."

"Tanisha, thank you. I will be there shortly."

"President," Regis rested her hands on the table.

"Secretary of Defense?"

"What if they don't want to assist us?"

"Then we will have a bigger problem."

"Yes, because we can't just swipe affluent people like them off the face of the planet no matter how much support we get from the public."

"Let's just see what's going on in their heads first, shall we?"

They both stood up and headed for the conference room. At the entrance, only him, the Vice President, Regis, General Perrara and a handful of assistants were allowed in. The Press Secretary was already inside setting up to conduct the questioning. The President surveyed the occupants sitting further in on the other side of the long table. He shook his head in amazement.

The supermodel sat in boredom since her commlink and tablet were confiscated while the famous actor drummed his fingers annoyingly on the top of his thighs. It made very little sound but the motion was distracting. A world-renowned center for the WNBA glared at him from the opposite end. Opera Singer Hagen was the picture of perfection and calm with his arms rested across his chest. One of the rock stars was a bit fidgety while the other appeared to be thinking, his brow scrunched up.

"Good evening, everyone." The President greeted them trying to sound as cheerful as possible. "I do apologize for dragging you from your events and to the White House, but I assure you it is of great national security."

"You meant planetary, don't you?" The famous actor stated. "It's not about one country or another. The whole planet is going to war, right?"

Hagen's head snapped up to attention. The President saw caution spread across his face. It was clear they were supposed to stay under wraps and the actor did not comply. Even the supermodel raised an eyebrow at his remarks.

"Well. Since you understand, let me get to the chase."

"Yes, please do," Hagen insisted.

"We brought you here because even with the Karysilan's help, we are at a loss. Our technology is not advancing fast enough and our soldiers needed DNA modification to be on a subpar level as our alien friends. We need more variety of fighting skills."

Silence went on for what seemed like an hour, but only a few minutes had passed before Hagen spoke up.

"Then my commanders and myself cannot help you."

"What?" The President was incredulous.

"I am the Commander of the Relliant Command Fleet, and these two," he pointed down to Bree and Craig, "are my second in command."

"Take them into custody," Regis barked.

"Stay that order!" The President countered.

In the same moment, Hagen raised one hand and said, "Wait." It was not loud but it was a command that was obeyed out of fear. He leaned forward. "As much as we enjoy being on Earth and have no intention of destroying it, our leader has spoken. We cannot go against him without a plan."

"So," the President echoed, stepping forward. "You mean your race does not agree with your General about this war?"

The doors opened while Hagen was in the middle of his sentence and Darnizva marched in. His cloak was undone at the waist and flowed behind him.

"Of course not. No matter how ruthless their race is, this is going a bit too far."

"Captain," Hagen nodded at him.

"Commander."

Secretary Regis was left standing in the middle of the room dumbfounded. She couldn't believe her people just obeyed an alien enemy over her orders. Defeated, she motioned for them to stand down even though they already had.

"Can't your people reason with him?" The President asked.

"Reasoning with General Tartha is like arguing with an infant." Hagen replied.

"Not to mention he has only been General for a little over two centuries." Darnizva added. "He is still trying to assert his power."

Regis turned to the super model.

"What race are you then?"

She sighed loudly and sat up a little in her seat.

"I am Karysilan. I am still a youngster though and have not had much combat experience. This was my first battle, thus…" she circled a finger in the air and slumped back into the back of the chair.

"And you?" Regis eyed Chasner.

"Hmm…" he breathed and glanced at Darnizva. "Should I really?"

"I think you should, considering how rare it is to see

one of your kind."

"You mean, considering we are nearly extinct due to all the wars?" He pressed his hands flat into his thighs and looked up at Regis. "I am a Chombrazen. We are not a warrior race or anything like that. Of course, we can defend ourselves."

"Not warriors, yet their expertise in combat is of the highest standard." Hagen interjected.

Their attention went to the WNBA player. She huffed and crossed her arms. "I am also Karysilan."

"That leaves you, son." The President referred to the seventh alien in the room who kept his presence to nearly zero.

The man sat legs crossed in a perfect posture, wearing vintage corduroy pants and a screen-printed shirt with a rainbow on it. In society, he was a well-known gay reality star. His hair was the color of brown sugar and cut short. He turned his head slightly to address them.

"I am what they call a Planetary Litigator." His gaze went back to the far wall even as the other aliens and Darnizva gasped in fear.

"What?" The President asked as he and the Vice President looked at each other. "What does that mean? Why are you all scared to death?"

"A Litigator? Here?" The super model cringed, scooting her chair farther away from the table. She wasn't alone in that act.

"What's a Litigator?" The President snapped. Darnizva turned to him, eyes wide in disbelief.

"Remember how we said there may be Senigrankes on Earth?"

"You mean the flesh eaters?" The Press Secretary screeched as he backed into the nearest wall. Everyone standing took a step back except Regis.

"Yes. Well, there is another equation with that race.

Some of them evolve into Litigators. They can literally negotiate with a planet and change its axis or the weather, or the terrain. The results can either be beneficial or catastrophic, depending on the Litigator's intent."

"Oh, so they evolve from eating people then?"

The humans breathed a sigh of relief.

"Oh, I still eat," the Litigator said softly, eyeing one of the Vice President's assistants. The young man nearly ran behind his colleagues for shelter from his gaze.

"Okay," The President nodded. "So, what's the giant issue?"

"Let me ask you, Mr. President, as I know your kind must take rudimentary science classes in your early years. What happens to the Earth if it shifts off its axis?" Hagen asked.

The entire room was silent again as every human in the room contemplated the answer. Finally, an aide raised their hand and replied, "Total destruction?"

"Correct. The last thing you want is a Litigator who can communicate and monkey with your planet." Hagen said. The Litigator clapped three times slowly and locked eyes with him.

"You haven't done anything while on Earth, have you?" The Vice President inquired.

"If I had, you would have known. I have no intention of using my power until it is deemed necessary."

"You make it sound like it's inevitable," Regis snorted.

"It is. The Relliants will not leave this planet in great shape and it may need to be terraformed all over again."

"Oh, dear God," The Vice President seemed to sway and was helped to a chair.

General Perrara sat listening the whole time, taking in every word and analyzing them. He agreed with the Litigator. Earth would not be left unscathed. Certain bits of information made him curious and while the assistants focused on the Vice President, he finally spoke up.

"When you say, you're just a youngster, Mrs. Antona, how old are we talking?"

"In Earth years, I am one hundred and eighty."

"You're joking?" Regis gasped.

"That's the equivalent of a twenty something in human terms." Darnizva added.

"How so?" Perrara asked. "Please, enlighten us."

"Our race and many of the others have a longer life span than humans. A fifty-year-old in our race would be like a sixteen-year-old. When they reach the age of one hundred, they are assigned to the military and are more like eighteen. One hundred marks adulthood."

"Which is debatable when you think of some warriors who do not act their age." Hagen retorted and stared at Darnizva.

"So, your front line consisted of mainly young ones, fresh out of the academy?"

"Sort of like that, yes."

"The same applies to your races as well?" He asked the others and they nodded. "Which means, and I am not trying to be insulting, you are on the low end of the totem pole."

"None taken. You are correct. All the ships that crashed on your planet are under my command as the first line of defense."

"Sacrificial lambs." Perrrara blurted out. "I also remember General Tartha saying something about you opening a pathway and that's why other races are here. How does that work?"

"Travel through the galaxies is done with what you might call portals. They can cross space and time seamlessly." Hagen interrupted to explain. "Most of the destinations are already plotted but occasionally a new pathway is created and opens a new portal. What Darnizva did was reckless but it was the only way to save his battalion."

"Well, I can't fault him for that," Perrara replied.

He would have done the same.

"You opened a portal and jumped to a random coordinate, didn't you?" Darnizva crossed his arms and frowned, nodding. "At the rate of speed those ships were going, there was no way they could avoid a crash landing being so close to your orbit as they came out of the vortex."

"Thank you for that," Perrara said. "Now, can we negotiate support from all of you since you seem to like being on our planet?"

"When you say negotiate?" Chasner asked, dubiously.

"I mean, what can we do for each other? Darnizva said your race is unparalleled in fighting skills. We could use a different approach."

"Who is assisting in your training of human soldiers now?" Bree spoke up.

"Oh, that would be Lieutenant Sspark of the League."

Hagen turned around to look at Darnizva, confusion on his face. Bree's lips went tight and Craig let out a laughed. The Litigator uncrossed his legs and leaned forward.

"You have a Sphere wielder," he started, "No, an immature and arrogant Sphere wielder, training your troops to fight against the Relliants?"

"Is that a problem? Darnizva assures us he is the best candidate for the job."

"Darnizva is also still a youngster and Sspark is even younger. Both are irresponsible." Hagen interjected.

"I am going to concur. A great and powerful warrior Sspark is, but a great teacher, he is not." The Litigator added.

General Perrara glanced over at Darnizva who was visibly angry. He knew all too well what happens when you put unseasoned soldiers in charge of their own battalion and things go bad. He could see the frustration in the young Captain's expression.

"Let's not be too harsh," Perrara suggested. "They are doing the best that they can, given the situation. I commend them both for trying to help us and getting authorization from General Phalkar."

"What you're saying is there really isn't any help. Phalkar will not lift a finger to aid this planet so it is all on Darnizva to fix this mess." Hagen shook his head in disgust.

"To throw your own child to the wolves and see if it can fend for itself against the Relliant Command Fleet is horrible." Antona exclaimed.

"I keep hearing about this Command Fleet," Perrara gestured to Hagen, "the one you command, right?" Hagen nodded. "Why is that so significant?"

"Because," Hagen locked his gaze on the General. "The Relliance can save its energy and manpower by sending its most powerful fleet to do the dirty work."

"Just so you know, General," Darnizva regained his voice. "the Relliance does not have civilians. The children are raised in the military until they are old enough to start training."

Perrrara wasn't sure he understood but the implication was frightening. Before he could ask for clarification, Hagen did so.

"Our entire planet's population aged fifty and above is our military."

"And your population is?"

"Nearly twelve billion."

Perrara watched Secretary Regis take ill with the information. He could taste bile creeping up in his throat and he forced it back down. "So that means you have…"

"Any infinite amount of ships," Darnizva finished for him.

"And the Command Fleet?"

"We are five ships. But we can do the same amount of damage as a five hundred vessel fleet. That is why we are usually sent when the General doesn't feel the need to bother with a full armada."

"You mean," President barely contained his rage, "we are not even worth going toe to toe with? We're just some ants for him to step on?"

"Essentially," Hagen looked at him, "Yes."

General Perrara could see clearly now and the information solidified his resolve when he, along with Professor Makoto, laid plans to create a new organization. It was also clear that five of the seven aliens in the room were the cream of the crop. All the others were just random visitors or young soldiers.

"Now that we have all of that out of the way." He saw the President prepared to say something and held his hand up. "I know you are angry sir, but let's put that aside for a moment." He turned back to the aliens. "Do we have a deal?"

"I explained to you earlier, we cannot help you," Hagen said pointing at himself and his two commanders.

"Of course, you can," Darnizva smiled. "I won't tell if you don't."

The humans all looked at Hagen, Bree and Craig. Even Chasner and Antona seemed intrigued. Perrara watched a sinister smile creep on the Litigator's face. Hagen was struggling with his decision but Bree was not.

"Agreed." Bree stated.

"You do not get to go against my command!" Hagen exploded.

"Are you going to say no?"

Hagen slammed his fists on the table and put his head in his hands. He turned his head towards Bree who sat with the full intent of going ahead with or without him. Lifting his head, he again found Perrara's gaze and replied, "Agreed."

"Sspark will not be happy," Craig chuckled. "He does not like his parade being marched on, especially by us."

"Well, Mr. President," Perrara announced, "We have new allies."

The President gave him a dirty look. The fact they weren't worthy adversaries still stung.

⤳

Darnizva threw himself on his bed facedown and breathed in the sterile cleanliness of the coverings. He had not been to sleep in days, which was nothing new if he were engaged in battle, but his exhaustion stemmed from trying to keep Lieutenant Sspark from causing a planetary disaster during training sessions. To add insult to injury, he found that some of the humans were doing ignorant, selfish things instead of figuring out a way to survive.

Are all our efforts to help save them for nothing?

The doors to his quarters opened and he turned to see Sspark enter without asking, yet again. It was getting tiresome arguing with him about it so Darnizva didn't move to acknowledge his presence. Sspark was not to be ignored and stepped onto the bed, his stare boring holes in the back of Darnizva's head.

"What are you, a child?" Darnizva snapped as he turned his head towards him. "Get off my bed." Sspark tilted his head. "Or do you wish to lie with me instead of my father." Darnizva flopped over onto his back and smiled up at him. Sspark in turn gave a look of disgust and stepped down onto the floor.

"I would never let you touch me."

"That's a bit harsh is it not?"

"I despise you with every fiber of my being."

"Yet, you never tell me why that is."

Sspark glanced back at him briefly then sat on the cushioned window seat. Darnizva followed and sat facing the Lieutenant whose sparkling tunic nearly hurt his eyes. He never understood why Sspark insisted on that design of body tunic.

"Are you being all moody again about those fledgling humans?" Sspark started.

"If you must know, yes. I think we need a better plan than helping them build better weapons and teaching them how to fight."

"Really, Darnizva, what is our stake in all this?"

"What do you mean?"

"Yes, your ships crash landed on their planet, but it was not intentional. WE do not owe them anything outside of an apology. Are we going to stay here?"

"No, of course not."

"Then why? We help them. They win, end of story. We help them, they lose. End. Of. Story. We go home either way"

"And if other races invade because we opened the pathway?"

"Not our concern, Darnizva. They will have to defend their planet just like every other in the galaxy."

"Sspark."

"Hmm?" Sspark turned his gaze from the viewing window to Darnizva's cinnamon colored eyes lock with his.

"It infuriates me when you're right."

"I know, Darnizva, I know." Sspark nodded twice then smacked Darnizva's hand away when he tried to move a lock of his hair. "Don't touch me."

Darnizva let out a small laugh and sat back against the wall. He liked toying with Sspark but eventually, he would not tolerate the standoff much longer.

⤜

"Commander Gragor reporting in," Geoffrey Hagen announced as he bowed slightly forward, one arm with a closed fist across his chest. He peeked at General Tartha sitting in the command center of the Relliant mother ship. So much activity buzzed around him yet he paid no heed.

"Closer, Commander." Tartha spoke as he motioned with two fingers, his eyes never leaving the screen in front of him. "I prefer not to yell today."

Hagen stepped closer and stood still, awaiting the General's orders. This was a war he did not condone and resented having to use his Command Fleet, but the General's demands were absolute and he couldn't deny it. He glanced behind him to make sure Bree and Craig were paying attention.

"I need your insight on this planet and its resources before I make my final decision. What are your thoughts, Commander?"

"Somewhat primitive, they deplete their resources at an alarming rate and climates are unstable, changing often. Though, they are consistent annually."

"Is it worth taking over?" This time Tartha turned his entire body towards Hagen and stood. He was shorter yet his presence was larger than life.

Hagen used all his training to not cringe away from him. Something about the young General frightened not just him, but the entire race.

"I believe we can use the planet's resources better than the humans and there is plenty of space. Our people could finally spread out."

"So, the humans are not necessary. If anything, they're a disease."

"I wouldn't go so far…."

"I've decided then," Tartha cut him off. "If by some miracle they survive, we will negotiate that a third of our population be allowed to transplant on Earth."

Hagen could feel the tension ease up in the room, especially from his two second in commands. He was about to reply when Tartha continued.

"If they lose, of course." He eased back down in his seat and folded his hands in his lap. "We will raze the entire planet surface and a different planet within this solar system should be found to inhabit."

Any paler and Bree would have become invisible. Even Hagen felt the color drain from his own body. To destroy a planet and an entire race because you can't have it was, at best, childish and not part of the warrior code. It was decisions like these that made Relliants question General Tartha's leadership and at the same time fear him. A silence had filled the control room and Hagen realized that everyone on deck had stopped moving to stare at General Tartha.

"Do you not approve?" He barked at them loudly.

The soldiers resumed their tasks.

"There is no reason to our plan, General," Hagen protested.

"There is reason," Tartha snapped, "It is as I say." He tapped the screen in front of him and a hologram of the solar system sprang up above him. "Make sure you are ready when the time comes. I want you and your high officers to report here every five years. Understood?" He glanced over at Hagen and then his two officers.

"As you please, General." Hagen bowed again, fist to chest and headed out of the command deck with Bree and Craig in tow.

He kept his mouth clenched shut all the way to the transport room. A burning sensation formed in the pit of his abdomen and he knew how angry he had become. This was not how it was supposed to go.

Back on Earth, transported to his personal chamber, the three sat down mulling over the General's orders. Bree shucked off his cloak and sat upright on the edge of the sofa.

"I will not let this planet be destroyed." He declared.

Stunned, Craig and Hagen stared at him and seeing his resolve they both nodded with heavy heads. The implication of becoming traitors and fighting their own race was not a fond idea. They just needed a plan that would shield them.

"Agreed," Hagen responded. "But, first you need to be up to par. If you are not at full strength, then all is for nothing."

"So," Craig exhaled and spread his arms across the back of the sofa. "When do we brainstorm this bat shit crazy plan?"

SEPARATE AGENDAS

Professor Bartley was not happy with the talent data for Bi-Genetics presented by the testing lab. So far, it showed his facility had the most talented and deadliest than the others. He found this hard to believe with his knowledge of Professor Makoto's and Professor's not so well-known assistants.

Do the world leaders think I'm so gullible as to think my facility was somehow special?

He asked himself this while pacing his quarters.

On the other side of the bay windows, the labs were in full swing, it being after lunch hours. This was when most of the real work got done. From the corner of his vision, he saw a lab technician trying to get his attention. He went to his commlink which was blinking furiously and tapped to answer.

"Sorry to bother you, sir, but I sent a report to your station that may surprise you."

"Thank you. I will go over it in a moment and get back to you."

Bartley swiped his hand across his terminal and waited for the screen to fully load. Finding the file, he tapped its icon and two different reports were displayed. He began reading both, switching his eye sight from one screen to the other because he had a feeling the two were related.

The first report came from his source in Italy about Kevin Lang's little venture. It listed in detail the information about the new Terror Base and the timely intervention of the Organics. Professor Bartley nearly gagged as his lunch partially crept up his esophagus before receding. The second report was even more disturbing. It seemed General Hoskins had a friend in the facility business and created his own Bi-Genetic manufacturing plant. He called them Primers and they were for sale to the highest bidder then custom engineered with a prime directive implanted, hence the name.

Shaking his head in disgust, Bartley tried not to be surprised. General Hoskins always had a level of disdain for Bi-Genetics and this was just his way of contributing to his own cause. He would not be the first or even the last to come up with something disgusting. There were bound to be many more horrors to come before Bi-Genetics were fully accepted. This caused the professor to decide to leave his enclosed quarters and consult with his trusted group of scientists in person.

"I'm coming down," Professor Bartley announced into the commlink. He saw every area in his view perk up and start to panic.

"Of course, sir. We will be waiting," the lab technician responded.

Leaving the room, he entered the clear, shatter proof elevator directly attached to his entryway and swiped his key card. He didn't like being outside of his bubble and everyone knew that. Whenever he did, it was for something important and protocols were activated to ensure his unobstructed passage through the facility. The elevator doors opened and he swiftly made his way to the boardroom.

A long white oval table sat in the center of the room, seeming to float due to the white floors and walls. Sixteen scientists sat around it with the seat at the head empty for him. He strolled in and sat. His expression must have looked dire because some of his colleagues grimaced at the sight.

"Ladies, Gentlemen. We have a serious problem." They all nodded in agreement. "Please, give me your insight on these matters."

"Well, first off," his bioengineer, Doctor Harris started. "There's nothing we can do to stop it because we do not have direct transport access to either of them. The only thing we can do is expand our protection of these Primers."

"As for the new Terror base, now called Ortega City, Metropolis," Professor Graham added. "We have no way of gaining an audience with the one running that installation. If we can establish that, it would let us gauge the situation."

"None of these idiotic ventures help us win against a superior alien threat in less than three decades," Doctor Yan spoke up, slamming a fist on the table. Her glasses slid down her nose a bit from the impact. "What the hell are these people thinking?"

"I concur. And that asinine data about our facility having the largest number of high level Bi-Genetic talent. That's the biggest load of horseshit I've seen in a long while." Professor Vasence interjected, crossing his arms and leaning back in his chair.

"We need to get everyone focused back on the agenda at hand, which is the survival of the human race," Professor Bartley said.

"We could reach out to the military. Is there anyone viable we can discuss this with?" Doctor Harris asked, scanning the room for an answer.

"There is General Perrara," a scientist on the other side of the table replied.

"Hmph!" Doctor Yan snorted. "He also has his own agenda."

"Yes, but part of his agenda is saving Earth." Professor Vasence added.

Professor Bartley set one elbow on the table and rested his chin in his hand. A faraway look surfaced and he began to tap the table's edge with the fingertips of his other hand. His eyes started to narrow and he arched his back, stopping his tapping to scratch along the birth mark on his spine then resuming. Two tiny glints of yellow flashed in his pupils and disappeared in the same instant.

"I don't like our options, but we have to do some-thing," he finally spoke. "Talk with the General. See what he proposes." He stood, his colleagues following suit. "I'm going to lie down for a while."

As he exited the boardroom, the others sat back down to continue deliberation.

⤸

If there was one thing General Perrara learned in all his years in the military, it was to cover your ass and keep your enemies close. The scientists before him were by no means his enemy, but they had a different view-point than his, so there was potential. He had gotten the request for a sit down through the emergency channel of his commlink and after hearing the basics, agreed. Too many agendas not benefitting humanity could not be tolerated any longer with war coming in so short a time.

"So," he began. "Here we are trying to get everyone in sync and it's falling apart. Is there a way to locate this new facility of Hoskins? The President, as well as a few world leaders, would love to have a chat with him."

"I want his head on stick," Doctor Yan spat.

"Yes, well, we all want that."

Perrara took a quick glance at the mini skirt riding

dangerously high up Doctor Yan's thighs.

"We want your thought on how this war is going to go before we start implementing plans that may not bring good results." Professor Vasence said.

"Hmm. Let's see. Introduction of alien DNA strands have the effect of slowing the aging process to a crawl. This is great because the soldiers we are in the process of training now will still be practically the same age in forty years since inoculation."

"True, we have seen that with our research as well." Doctor Harris said.

"That being said, it's a no brainer that their children, and maybe grandchildren for some, will also be fighting this battle alongside them."

"I didn't even think about that," Professor Vasence sighed.

"The trick is one, finding the right mates for these soldiers and two, having a training base large enough, yet capable to remain hidden."

"And?" Doctor Yan inquired. "I am sure you have already started to put your plan in motion. What's in place, so far?"

She's a sharp one, General Perrara thought.

"I have been coordinating with Professor Makoto of Japan and we are in the throes of our creation we call The Shadow Organization."

"Who are their trainers?" Doctor Harris asked.

"Darnizva helped us make contact with four beings who have very different fighting skills and a better handle on combat than we do."

"Not Karysilans?" Professor Vasence balked.

"No. I requested that they not be. Of course, they are learning some of the ancient sword techniques and implementing them in the training since there is something similar in their worlds." He chuckled and smiled.

"It was a stipulation of Professor Makoto's."

"All you need is for us to run our database and find all the correlating mates to ensure a better batch of soldiers when the war starts." Doctor Yan interrupted his reverie.

General Perrara looked up and straightened his posture. "Yes. That is correct."

"If we can get some offspring in the next two years, we may be able to have three generations." Professor Vasence spoke, stroking his chin.

"Oh, yeah! And an entire bloodline eliminated in one fell swoop!" Doctor Yan yelled.

"That is a major drawback," Perrara stated. "But, I don't plan on losing."

"We never do, General." Doctor Harris retorted.

END

EXCERPT FROM

CURVE OF HUMANITY
BOOK TWO

SHADOWMEN OBJECTIVE

PAVING A WAY

A group derived from the best spies on the planet converged on the bunker, forming a semicircle of vehicles around the front gate. They totaled nearly one hundred with five to six people per car. Each one had been blind-folded for the trip and none made any complaint about it. Because of their professions, they knew it came with the territory.

On the other side of the gate, General Perrara stood waiting for incoming. He had set up separate briefing rooms for when the groups were ushered into assigned sectors. These elites were going to be the organization's observers. Combat would be only when necessary but he brought them for their minds and intelligence. He figured this many would be a great start and could always add more if needed. They would have their fingers on the pulse of everything involved to ensure it all went smoothly.

The doors of all the vehicles were opened and the spies led out in single file through the main entrance. Some of them tilted their heads, others sniffed the air. Their body language suggested they were trying to get a feel for the location. One of the men had a wide grin.

"I know that smell. The desert is nice this time of year."

"At least there's air conditioning in this installation. Those units are humming along pretty good," a woman not far down from him added.

Perrara laughed inwardly. He expected nothing less from the handpicked candidates. The soldiers at the gate scanned the barcode each person wore on their wrist. Hana in his infinite wisdom had also suggested the protocol for checking them in. If Professor Makoto hadn't already claimed the beauty, he would have seriously thought about taking him.

He walked over to the soldier right inside the bunker and got close.

"Make sure you leave the blindfolds on even after they are secured. I don't want them to know anything until the time is right."

"Absolutely, sir. Are we going to give them some refreshments?"

"Now, how would it look if we denied people a drink in the middle of the desert?"

"Very good, sir. I'll get right on it."

As the soldier handed off his clipboard to his counterpart, General Perrara turned his attention back to the line of spies.

Welcome to a new era of counter intelligence.

The two spies sat side by side at a table in a small holding cell. A glass full of clear liquid was placed in front of each. Both leaned over and gave a sniff then smiled. They raised their glasses and toasted in unison.

"Prost!"

"Salud!"

The glasses now empty, they slammed them down on the table. Perrara gave them a round of applause as he sat in the chair across from them. He removed the hardcopy manila folder from under his arm and set it down in front of him.

"I hope that was to your liking. I sprung for the good stuff."

"I've had better, but it was still good," the Russian said.

"Not bad. Though I would have preferred some water," the Italian female replied.

"Vodka is water," the Russian protested.

"So." The woman adjusted in her seat. "Are we conducting this interview incognito?"

"My apologies," Perrara said. "I want to make sure you're on board before we start talking face to face."

"Understandable. This is something very big if you have spies from all over the world," the Russian stated.

"You could say that." General Perrara leaned forward and rested his forearms on the table. "I, along with Professor Makoto, am creating a new organization that answers to no government. We will be independent yet have power over everything. To do this, we need a network of intelligence that rivals any in the world. Agents who can work behind the scenes, not intervene or change outcomes unless absolutely necessary."

"To what end?" The woman asked.

"To win this war without having humankind becoming extinct." A deep silence filled the room. He continued. "This planet is a board with moving chess pieces. We want those capable of knowing what strategy is required to accomplish our goals."

"Vague, but I like it." The Russian smiled. "I'm in."

"I'm also intrigued. Count my expertise as yours. What are you calling this new order?"

General Perrara nodded to the soldiers guarding the door. They went over and removed the blindfolds. The two spies squinted to adjust their vision in the brightly lit room.

"The Shadow Organization."

He smiled as they also appeared to be amused by the name. Another round of Vodka was poured, this time one for him as well.

The communication monitor on Perrara's desk lit up with a phone and camera icon. He tapped the touch screen and Professor Makoto's face filled it.

"How did it go?"

"There were only a handful who declined."

"So, we're ready for phase one?"

"Getting the packets together as we speak. Hana is very resourceful."

He saw a hint of possessiveness creep up in the professor's eyes.

"Yes, he is." There was pause. "What about the training grounds?"

"Still working out the kinks. The indoor assessment looks promising. I believe if even a handful get through that obstacle course, we would have a good unit on our hands."

"Yes, but we need a hell of lot more than that."

"Don't take me so literally, Professor," Perrara laughed.

It was true in sense. The course was built to put a strain on all the senses. One wrong decision and the candidate could get seriously hurt. He had two medical wings set up on either side to ensure quick response. But, the professor was right. They had to get as many units as possible to plant inside the military ranks.

"Phase Two?"

"Still waiting on Professor Bartlett."

He knew what the doctor had been through and cursed the scientist who created the facilities. A lot of horrors happened in those places. None of it for the greater good of humanity. This time, the Bi-Genetics on his list would suffer for one that does. Bartlett's hesitation was not surprising.

"He's meticulous. Give him all the time he needs. He knows the deadline."

"I'm just anxious," Professor Makoto snapped.

"So am I. Let's have a little more patience."

Professor Makoto nodded.

"I hope to hear an update soon."

With that, the screen went blank and his screen saver resumed. General Perrara sighed and swung around in his chair to face the window. Night had fallen and the desert sky was full of stars. Mankind wanted so badly to reach further than their solar system but knowing what's out there, he wondered if that was the right answer. Compared to the aliens in their midst, humans were like insects. And not the resourceful kind.

Can we even win?

ABOUT THE AUTHOR

Hi there. I'm Maquel A. Jacob.

I have had a passion for the written word since the age of seven, reading everything I could get my grubby little hands on which included encyclopedias and the thesaurus. At twelve, I had my first encounter with a Stephen King novel and was hooked. I then became inspired to write my own brand of fiction. Combining multiple genres to keep things interesting.

I am a HUGE Anime fan, love a great bottle of wine and rock out to heavy metal music. Green and lush Oregon is where I currently reside spinning imaginary worlds in my head and daydreaming.

For cool limited-edition Swag, updates, FREE short stories, Newsletters

...and more

Visit: http://www.maquelajacob.com/

Like Maquel A. Jacob on Facebook

Follow on Tumblr and Twitter @MaquelAJ1

Also find me on Goodreads

MAJart Works on Instagram

CPSIA information can be obtained
at www.ICGtesting.com
Printed in the USA
JSHW021418170622
27188JS00002B/130